Cowgirl

CRAZY

A Standalone Novella

Bad Girls: Book Two

By Jennifer Labelle

Cowgirl Crazy

Copyright © 2018 by Jennifer Labelle.
All rights reserved.
First Print Edition: December 2018

Limitless Publishing, LLC
Kailua, HI 96734
www.limitlesspublishing.com

Formatting: Limitless Publishing

ISBN-13: 978-1-64034-499-0
ISBN-10: 1-64034-499-3

Dedication

For my other half,

You've been lighting my way out of the dark for all these years. Happily-ever-afters really do exist and because of your love and patience I was blessed early on, so thank you for that.

Prologue

Epilogue from: Chasing Butterflies Bad Girls: Book One

The self-serve gas station was deserted as he filled up his motorcycle, except for the attendant behind the counter inside, waiting for him to pay up. Fuck, it was hot, and all he wanted was some food, a shower, and a comfortable bed to catch some Z's. It'd been a long trip but well worth the headache to get here. Sawyer was like a sister to all of them and Toby had sent him down here to keep an eye on things. They worried about her all alone in a place that held so many bad memories to keep her company.

He needed a change of scenery and this was his chance to start over.

He was done pumping and tightened his gas cap before he ran inside to get a move on. Baby girl was waiting for him and would probably be worried if he didn't show up soon. He straddled the bike, unhooked his helmet, and was about to put it on when a noise from across the street distracted him from his task.

The woman making the racket was short, stacked, and curvy in all the right places. Not his usual type, but she intrigued him none the less even from afar, so he thought *what the hell* and ran across the street to see what the matter was.

The woman was on the sidewalk in front of the store she'd just left and was quickly scrambling to get all her stuff back inside the sack she'd dropped by accident.

"Can I help you out over here?" He knelt down to get a better look at her haggard state. She was definitely anxious about something, but what? It hadn't taken long to find out once he paid better attention to the situation.

"I'm such a klutz sometimes, I swear," she mumbled, and finally looked up. "If you'd really like to help, you'll pass me my belongings before that old coot comes over. She's a gossip and I don't need the headache."

He looked behind him where she pointed to see a wrinkly old lady about two blocks away approaching quickly. "Whatever you say," he said and shrugged. He quickly helped her out, only to realize why she was so frantic as he was putting everything he'd found back in the bag she held out.

She looked innocent, but she was anything but. He quirked a brow in surprise to see a monstrous pink vibrator, some anal lube, and various other sex toys inside. He shifted when his dick got hard and nearly groaned. Clearly his cock had plans of its own.

"Brodie Mace, but my friends just call me Mace. And you are?" He held out his hand as he introduced himself and waited for her to do the same.

Her face flushed and she quickly stuffed the bag back into her oversized purse to hide the evidence of what he had seen inside, but little did she know he had a photographic memory. Oh, this woman was something all right. Someone he wouldn't mind getting to know better. Innocent on the outside but clearly something wild in the sheets.

His kind of woman, after all.

"Oh, I'm Becca. Becca Everett." She finally shook his hand just as the little old lady caught up to them.

"I saw you dropped the bags, dear, and I rushed right over to make sure you were all right."

The nosy little bitty eyed him up and he sighed. "Brodie Mace, a pleasure to meet you, Ma'am." He shook her hand too and he could feel Becca's eyes studying him, so he looked at her. "From what I could tell, it was all an accident, but Becca here is fine, and all her stuff has been accounted for." He smiled when she blushed, a deeper red this time. He decided to save her yet again. "Well, I'm running late so I've got to get going." He addressed the old woman. "Would you like some help crossing the street?" He didn't have a clue where she was headed but held out his arm for her to accept or not regardless.

When she did, Becca looked relieved. "See you around, Becca," he said, and he meant it. She was such a conundrum and it piqued his curiosity. Plus, she kind of owed him one and he was hoping to cash in with dinner sometime or something.

"Oh, thank you, dear." The old lady patted his arm once they were across and he quickly bid her adieu without even getting her name.

Soon, he was on the road again, helmet on his head, sunglasses shading his eyes, and the rumble of his motorcycle vibrating his ass. He was on his way and the new scenery already held promise.

Fifteen minutes later, Sawyer was running out of her house as he shut down the bike. She hugged him something fierce as soon as she could and he laughed while he hugged her back. It was so good to see her again and looking so happy too. It was a pleasant surprise. "How you doing, squirt?"

"Ha, ha," she said, flipping him the bird. "It's good to see you, Mace. Took you long enough."

"Tell me about it," he teased. "I need food, a good wash, and some sleep, but before any of that, I need you to tell me more about the lovely Becca Everett."

Sawyer smiled, her eyes lit up, and she rubbed her hands together. He knew that look, because she'd given it to him the last time she tried to set him up with someone. Only this time, he didn't mind. Not one bit.

Chapter One

Becca

For curious minds,

Once upon a time in the Hill Country of Texas, there lived a little girl who had it all. She had loving parents and a bratty but lovable little brother, and she still believed in fairy tales. Then as the years passed by, life happened. She had to grow up well before her time, her parents died, and she endured much heartache as she struggled to raise her brother on her own, but they'd made it.

Now, as an adult, she knew better. Fairy tales were meant for movies and romance novels, and although she would love nothing more than to indulge in the fantasy of a happily-ever-after when it came to love, in reality, it simply didn't exist. Not in her life, not for a very long time.

And still, life went on. This woman became a

successful career woman while her bratty but lovable baby brother was now a college man on his own. She was proud, strong, and busy. Very, very, busy, spending her days not only running her business, but maintaining her household, indulging in her art when time permitted, and being a part of town committees to keep up appearances. Who is this girl I write of you might ask? Well, let me tell you. She's me, Ms. Anonymous.

wink

A lot of you have written in to ask about me, so I'll give you another hint.

I'm a good ol' southern girl, born and raised, conservative on the outside, but also a lil' lonely and wild deep down. I'm someone you probably walk by every day without a second glance, and I haven't been on a good date in years. Hence, all of this self love y'all.

Welcome back to Cowgirl Crazy, this is the blog where anything goes. Try to keep things respectful at all times. You've got questions and I'll do my best to answer. This is a place to let loose, fulfill your curiosities, and enjoy the temporary escape. Who I am isn't very important in the grand scheme of things, right?

Now, down to business, the fun part. Last week I was asked in the comments to review The Satisfier Pro. So here goes...

This clit stimulator is small with smooth curves and it has a nice silky silicone tip. It comes with eleven different unique suction sensations, a waterproof design, and conveniently it's equipped with a charger for your ongoing enjoyment.

So, if you're looking for a great toy that isn't loud, is very easy to clean, and seriously does give toe-curling orgasms then this is the one for you. This Cowgirl gives it a 4.5 out of 5 thumbs up. I'll post links in the comments section, or you can head down to your nearest sex toy shop to purchase one. Men, your ladies will thank you, and ladies let me just tell you...whew!

The name really does speak for itself. The Satisfier Pro is really a pro at satisfying.

So, while I fan myself off, I'd also like to give a shout out to Mr. Tall, tanned, inked, and sexy for being the highlight in my fantasies while I tested out this product. *Grins* I'll tell y'all more about our encounter in next week's post. At that time, I'll be taking more review requests. So, think about it, make it sexy, and I'll look forward to seeing what peaks your curiosity once again. Remember, I've got a list of products to choose from already, and if what you desire isn't on there just let me know and I'll see what I can do.

Pleasurable encounters and pleasant dreams,
Your number one Cowgirl Crazy lady,
E.
XO

***

Rebecca (Becca) Everett sighed as she shut down

her computer and got up to put away her latest parcels. Inside, there was a giant pink vibrator with a mechanical tongue attached for double the pleasure, as promised on the box, and she hoped it was as good as advertised. There were a couple of tubes of lube, nipple clamps, and anal beads inside too. She took her newest additions and opened the big trunk at the bottom of her closet to throw them inside with the rest, and she shook her head in disbelief before a giggle escaped.

I can't believe this is what my life has come to.

She'd started the blog as a way to open up, to get out of her comfort zone, while also keeping her anonymity, and it was booming with followers, so much so that she'd become sponsored. It was amazing how many people connected through it.

Her overflowing adult toy box kept on growing thanks to all of the companies that sent her the sex toys free of charge in exchange for a little advertising. It was a good gig too, seeing how lonely she'd been feeling lately.

It had been eleven months, three days, and Lord only knew how many hours since the last time she'd been with a man in the flesh. She nearly groaned thinking about it. She had a full life, though, a crazy busy one to help pass the time, but every now and again, she longed for something more than what she had. The page was amazing, all hers, and like-minded women enjoyed it too. It wasn't your usual blog, but it was definitely getting recognition, mostly positive.

The loud rumble of a motorcycle outside startled her and she bit her lip as she walked to the window to catch a glimpse of it.

Hot damn!

She squealed and fled to the mirror to check her appearance.

*Speaking of Mr. Fantasy Man...*he was about to make an appearance in a minute.

Brody Mace, just Mace to his friends, drove by her house every day to get to the house he rented from her good friend, Sawyer.

Sawyer Maddox had moved back to town after the tragic passing of her sister, rekindled a relationship with her long-lost love, and became one of Becca's tenants, once she'd opened Mad Ink. Currently located in a commercial property she owned, and they'd hit it off instantly. The tattoo parlor had been quite a success too. Hence, the sudden arrival of Mace, a sexy tattooist with a body made of sin, and according to Sawyer, he was also single, had a heart of gold, and was totally badass too.

Speaking of, the total package had just turned into her driveway with Sawyer in tow to see...her.

A cloud of dust and debris followed the drool-worthy man sitting atop the equally sexy machine making all that noise. There was just something about a man on a bike that did it for her, hell it probably did something to the entire female species. She snorted and turned to leave her home office to get the door.

Here goes nothin'.

"Hey, Becca," Sawyer said as she practically skipped up the porch and enveloped her into a hug. "I asked Mace to stop by, so I can invite you to join us tomorrow night."

"Oh?" She lifted a brow. "What's up?" Becca stepped back as Mace joined them and gestured for them to come inside with a sweep of her hand.

"Well, now that Mace has settled in, a bunch of us were going to meet at Tipsy's Bar to celebrate his welcome to Kerrville, and my engagement to Jagger." Sawyer jumped with excitement as she showed off her new ring and Becca joined in on the excitement with a squeal as she hugged her again.

"Oh, my God. Congratulations!"

Mace chuckled and a whole new excitement started to build. Becca fidgeted to ease the awkwardness. Damn that man and her overactive libido, which increased since their run in a couple of weeks ago. "I also have a favor." He stated and she took a deep breath before speaking to hopefully keep the nervous tremble out of her voice.

"Excuse me?" She was dumbfounded as she looked between her friend and her walking fantasy. It must have been the expression on her face because Sawyer and Mace both smiled at her widely.

"We'll get to that in a minute," Sawyer remarked and brushed her hand in the air like it wasn't a big deal. "I still need an answer, tomorrow night, please say yes," she pleaded, and Becca sighed because she was more of a homebody and everyone knew it, in this case, though...

"I have a committee meeting tomorrow night, so as long as it doesn't run too late, I don't see a problem with it." She shrugged. "What time would you like to meet up?"

***

Mace

That a girl!

Mace studied the brunette beauty and became more and more intrigued every time he saw the woman. Today she had her long dark hair up in a messy bun with tendrils of hair falling out along the column of her slender throat, and he wondered if it was as soft as it looked. He shoved his hands in his front pockets, so he wouldn't reach out and test it for himself. She wore cut off jean shorts that fell a few inches above the knee, and a form-fitting white tank that showed off her curves so damn well he was sporting a semi already, and he'd only been there for about a minute.

The two women were talking beside him, so it gave him a second to take in his surroundings. She lived in a nice two-story ranch style home with a large white wraparound porch on the outside. He'd rode by every day to get to and from work seeing as they were neighbors and all, but this had been his first trip inside. They all stood near the entryway so there wasn't much but a big closet, a bench, a few pictures on the wall, and some hardwood floors to see so it didn't give him much to go by in terms of Becca herself.

He'd asked Sawyer about her a few times, starting on his very first day after he'd helped the brunette vixen put away some stuff she'd dropped from her shopping bag after trying to hastily avoid a nosy old lady. The pink vibrator he noticed in those items just happened to be an added bonus, at least for him. It seemed the lovely Ms. Everett had a naughty side despite her good girl persona, and she really was good people from what he could gather.

So far, he'd learned Becca liked to keep busy. She'd not only raised her kid brother after their parents died, but she also owned real estate and worked on the committee for the Kerrville Arts and Cultural Center. She was friendly, beautiful, and according to Jagger, Sawyer's new fiancé Becca had been through a lot when she was younger, so he'd better tread carefully. He was pretty sure he'd meant that as a warning to not break her heart, not as a warning to stay away.

Mace tuned into the conversation again just as Sawyer excused herself to use the bathroom. So, she was all his now, for a couple of minutes anyway.

Becca cleared her throat and blushed a pretty shade of pink when it became just the two of them in the entryway, and he winked at her for an added effect.

"H-how rude of me. Can I offer you something to drink?" She gestured behind her and looked everywhere but directly at him. She turned around and headed down the hall.

"Sure, sweetness." Mace chuckled. Man, this chick was cute, especially when she got shy on him. He followed behind her until they entered the kitchen and he whistled. "Nice place you got here." The space was bright with lots of big windows, the hardwood floors continued into this space. The dark wood accentuated the light cabinetry throughout, there was a large island in the middle and the granite countertops were immaculate. They were light but had swirls of black and gray, and was that sparkles in the stone? *Shit!* Girly, feminine, pretty, just like the woman who chose them for the design. "I may need your help down the road on Sawyer's place. You know to give me some advice on decorating and *shi*…stuff." He shrugged, now that the squirt moved in with Jagger he had the place to himself and part of his contribution for staying there was to fix the place up for her. It needed a lot of work.

"Thank you!" Becca smiled as she opened the fridge. "I've got a pitcher of sweet tea, milk, water, and coffee?"

"Water's just fine." he said as he leaned against the counter across from her. She bent over to reach into the fridge to get it, and he took the opportunity to admire her firm ass while she did it too.

"So, is that the favor?" she asked, as she stood, nudged the door shut with her hip, and tossed him a bottle of the cold clear liquid.

"Say what?"

"The favor you mentioned earlier. Was it for me to help you decorate the house?" She lifted an eyebrow and waited for him to respond.

"Not even close." He smiled. "Sawyer mentioned you might have some free space for me to use as storage to house one of my babies until I get the garage finished. It'll probably be only for a couple of months but…"

"Your babies?" she asked.

"Yeah, I've got a '68 Yenko I'm almost done restoring so I need a space big enough to accommodate. You got any?"

"I'm assuming a Yenko is a car?" She bit her lip in concentration as she thought about it.

13

"Yeah, babe." He shook his head, totally amused by that question. "It's a super modified Camaro, a sweet ride too besides my bike that is. Maybe I should take you out in it sometime?"

"You guys are adorable," Sawyer interrupted. She was leaning against the doorway watching the two of them with interest. "I've been here for a couple minutes already and neither one of you noticed me. I love it!" She clapped her hands together. "Speaking of love, Jagger just called, and he'll be here any minute to pick me up. Thanks for the ride, Mace, I'll catch up with you later. Becca, I will see you tomorrow, nine p.m." Sawyer blew Becca a kiss and hugged Mace goodbye. "Have fun you two!" She wiggled her eyebrows up and down with one last parting look and disappeared down the hallway. A minute later, they both heard the door close and Becca surprised him as she giggled.

"Gotta love her, I swear."

"She's something all right," Mace replied, shaking his head before he continued. "You think the squirt is trying to play at matchmaker?"

"Ugh, I hope not." She fanned herself off as if she was hot suddenly. "Setups feel so forced to me. I'd prefer things to just happen naturally, no pressure, no expectations, and hopefully no disappointments. But maybe that's why it's been forever since I've dated anyone, because I tend to be picky."

"Oh, I don't know. It could work out." Mace shrugged and took a sip of the water she offered. "I think sometimes people could use a little push once in a while. You only live once, right? And, it never hurts to try, unless you're not feeling it. Then we've got a whole other problem."

"Let's just say I got tired of kissing a lot of frogs. This is all hypothetical though so there's no problem here. Now about your car…"

"Fair enough. We can always go slow," he interjected and nodded while he held her gaze with his own. "I'm cool with that because I gotta tell you, Ms. Everett, I've been thinking about you since our first run in and knowing Sawyer approves just makes it another win in my book. She's like a kid sister to me. So, I don't mind starting out as friends if that's what you need from me, but I am interested so know that going forward." Mace smirked. "Now close that pretty mouth before you catch flies. I can see that I've caught you off guard and I don't want you to feel uncomfortable around me—ever. Now about my car, you think you've got space for me?"

***

Becca

Whoa! Am I dreaming here? Somebody pinch me.

"You're amazing," Becca said as she came out of her moment of stupor. "Sort of all over the place, but um, thank you. You surprise me, and I like it, but it's sort of overwhelming at the same time. Being friends with you would be nice, the potential for more—let's just say you've got me intrigued. I have to get to know you better before I can take that plunge, so I appreciate the patience you've offered. As for space, I've got a place, it's close by, has plenty of room, and I think you'll like it. Care to take a look?"

15

"Hell yeah!" He motioned forward with his hand. "Lead the way, beautiful."

Oh, Lord, I was as nervous as a whore in church back there. Let's hope a little air will calm me some. Deep breaths, Becca, in and out nice and deep, he likes you!

They were outside now and it was hot as Hades. Her skin glistened from sweat and the tendrils of hair that fell from her bun were beginning to stick to her skin. Becca threw on a pair of shades and smiled as Mace went straight to his bike as if he planned on going somewhere for her to show the place she had in mind.

"No need, Tattoos, it's this way." She motioned with her thumb in the direction behind her and began walking backward.

"Tattoos?" He smirked and followed her.

"The ones you have are nice." She shrugged. "Are you not into nicknames?"

"Whatever you want, sweetheart, I'm game." Mace winked, and he caught up to her again. It was quiet for a moment as they walked side by side and then he asked, "So do you have any?"

"What, ink?" She shook her head. "Not yet, but Sawyer is wearing me down. Her art is amazing."

"It is, but she's not the only one who'd love to mark you." He chuckled. "Keep that in mind if you decide to take the leap. I'd love to show you some work I've done."

"I'll just bet." Becca teased and reached out to trace the lion tattoo on his right bicep before dropping her hand. Mace was full of tattoos and maybe one day she might explore them more up

16

close and personal. In the meantime, they'd arrived at the destination she had in mind.

She took a deep breath and gestured to the barn in the back of her house. It was empty, mostly used for storage, and had a space on the top where she liked to paint when she had a chance to. It was another one of her ways to escape her busy lifestyle. "So, this is it. It may need to be organized a little before you move your stuff in, but it should be enough room for you to work on your baby. The top loft however is off limits, my recreational space."

She took out her set of keys and unlocked the barn door. "If you like it, I can have a spare key ready for you by tomorrow." She kicked a box aside once she had the door open and went further inside with him, watching while he surveyed the place.

It wasn't much but the space would serve its purpose. Boxes were piled, a bit of old furniture was covered, and she had a couple of ATV's parked to the side from when she used to go mudding with Jett, her little brother. "I can have it cleaned out for you too, of course." Becca bit her lip and began to babble. "Most of the boxes can fit upstairs, the two four wheelers should be fine right there, and the few pieces of furniture can…"

"We'll work it out." He placed a hand on her shoulder and gently squeezed. "How much?"

"What?" she asked. Mace was so close now she could smell his aftershave. It was distracting, so she cleared her throat.

"The rent to use this place, how much?" he clarified, and she waved him off.

"We'll work something out." She repeated what

he'd been saying moments earlier. She was sharing the space with him after all. Her art studio was on the upper level, so she had to think about it. "You like it then?"

"Yeah, babe, I like it." The way he said it, and the way he was looking at her right then gave her goose bumps. It was like he was a man on a mission and she was his target.

"Good, because if not I can show you something else. This is the first place I thought of out of convenience. You know, seeing as you're close by and all." She gestured around them.

"It's good, Becca. Thank you." He took a step closer and lifted her chin with his finger, so she'd look at him again. "You're so beautiful, especially with a little extra color right there and there." He framed her face now and the thumbs on each hand moved across each of her cheeks back and forth. "So soft too." Becca's breath hitched as he moved his face closer. She closed her eyes the moment his plump lips kissed her forehead, and she let out a sigh when it ended all too quickly.

She licked her lips, and he zeroed in on the action. His thumb flicked over her bottom lip before he stepped back to give them both some much needed space. Her mind went to mush the moment he touched her, and she began to want things she had no business wanting, at least not yet.

Take it easy, Becca. You wanted slow remember? Her body didn't care. One touch from Mace and she ignited while her mind warned her to not rush into things. It had been way too long since she had gotten laid and as soon as Mr. Sexy Motorcycle Man left, she'd be going back upstairs to relieve some of the pressure between her legs. It was either that or a cold shower, which also held some appeal since it was so humid outside.

"S-so tomorrow night then?" she stuttered on her way out the door. Mace took the hint and followed her out.

"Yeah, I'll see you at Tipsy's." Mace bent forward to whisper in her ear, "Oh, and Becca, I can't wait."

She groaned. His warm breath against her ear made her shiver. Her nipples instantly puckered, and the very man that played her body without even trying very hard noticed with a smirk. Yep, she most definitely needed to make use of her favorite vibrator followed by a shower to cool down. This man was sex on legs and he knew exactly how he affected her.

Damn!

Chapter Two

Becca

Lusty Cowboy wrote:

"Thanks for the insight, my sexy E. With these clues I think I've finally figured you out."

As soon as her meeting with the arts and cultural center had finished, she rushed to the bathroom to change for her night out with Sawyer and the gang. It had been a long time since she went to a bar with friends, and she'd been looking forward to the celebration all day. On the way out, she decided to take a quick look at the blog from her phone to see if there were any requests yet for her next sexy adventure. Testing out sex toys and reviewing them had become a frequent part of her life this past year or so. It was also her biggest secret, and it kept things interesting in what was her otherwise boring day to day existence. One comment caught her attention and it gave her pause. She'd read Lusty Cowboy's comment over and over and it gave her the creeps.

Figured me out? What's that supposed to mean? Does he know who I am?

A million and one questions raced through her mind. She needed to be more careful.

"Hello dear, is everything all right?"

Becca turned as Mrs. Coulter spoke to her. The little old lady was endearing but was also a chatterbox, and a little nosy. The woman had good intentions most of the time but loved her gossip as well so there were situations where Becca had avoided her, especially when she tried to set Becca up with her grandson.

She suppressed a shudder.

Mrs. Coulter was also the lady rushing toward her the very first time she'd met Mace. Warmth spread through her just at the thought of him, and she could feel the color coming back to her face. The weird blog commenter would have to wait. He was new, and one reply on her last post didn't necessarily mean anything, right? Okay, he definitely gave off a creepy vibe with his wording, but her worry could be put off to another day over it.

Answer her Becca and hit the road. You have friends waiting.

"Just checking to make sure I didn't forget anything, but I'm good." She nodded. "Thank you for your concern though." Becca looped her arm together with the weathered woman's and guided them towards the exit. "Now, how about I walk you safely to your car?"

***

Tipsy's was a unique bar that catered to bikers and cowboys who were both badass and hard workers alike. From the moment you walked in it was a whole load of hunk as far as the eye could see. Who could complain? There was an old-fashioned wood bar in front, wooden floors, tables, and chairs. There was a a jukebox and had a half moon stage for live entertainment, and her favorite feature of course was the mechanical bull she knew she'd be riding before she left for the night.

"Becca!" Sawyer whistled from across the busy room and waved her hands in the air. *Oh, good Lord would you check that out? Hotness overload!*

Several tables were pulled together for their gathering with Sawyer and Jagger in the middle of everyone sitting lovingly side by side. The gorgeous bar owner and his lovely wife, Liam and Ava were there. Alex and Lena Dean sat by Jagger, and then there was Mace of course, who now had a woman hanging off his arm. They were both smiling, and her stomach felt queasy. She needed a drink ASAP. She held up a finger and pointed towards the bar, Sawyer nodded in understanding whispered something to her fiancé and joined her there.

"So glad you could make it," Sawyer said, and gave her a hug.

"Wouldn't miss it." Becca smiled. Her friend's excitement was contagious. She couldn't help but feel happy for her. "Can I buy you a drink?"

"How about a celebratory shot? Thanks to Liam and Ava we've got pitchers of beer at the table already, unless you'd prefer something else?" Sawyer replied.

"Beer is fine. I'll buy a round of shots for everyone though. What do you think they'd like?"

"How about a round of Hot Damn's? It's so good! It's got whisky, rum, vodka, and orange juice. It packs a punch, but it doesn't leave a raunchy aftertaste."

Becca nodded.

"What can I get for you?"

"Hey, Tonya I'll take a round of Hot Damn's for the table Liam's at."

"Becca Everett is that you?" Tonya the bartender smiled. "It's been a while, welcome back."

"Thank you." She smiled at the red-headed beauty in front of her.

"Shots for a party of eight, coming right up." Tonya walked off to make them.

"I guess I should have told her nine," Becca said, surprised to see that Mace was now alone at the table when she looked back. The woman he was talking to was nowhere around anymore.

"Why would you get nine? Unless you're planning on drinking two of em' but I wouldn't recommend it."

"Mace's date." Becca motioned towards the table. "When I walked in he was with someone."

Sawyer smiled knowingly at her. "Not a date. He came here with us and seemed to be really looking forward to seeing you tonight. I hear you've found him a great place for his car."

Becca shrugged like it wasn't a big deal, while her heart raced with excitement.

Not a date!

"Anyway, look at him." Sawyer said, "He's the odd one out right now and there are plenty of women in here who would love to keep him company. We're all couples at the table, and now that you're here we're evened out."

"This is not a date for us either," Becca blurted, blushing. "I am so out of the game. It's been way too long."

"Which is why you'd be so good for him." Sawyer gently squeezed her arm. "Mace is like family, and you're you. You know, kind of awesome, and definitely nothing like his usual girls. Trust me that is a good thing. I really think if you'd both give it a shot it'd be worth it. Anyone with eyes can see there's a certain spark between the two of you."

"Um…" She was speechless. "Thanks, I guess."

"Here you go!" Tonya set two shots in front of them. "Our waitress is bringing the rest to the table."

Becca nodded and handed Tonya enough money to cover the bill as well as a generous tip. Then she took a deep breath before she downed the shot for a bit of liquid courage. It seemed fate was steering her in the direction of a tempting, tattooed man who was not only sexy, but also caring, talented, and well…beautiful, both inside and out.

She just had to take the leap.

***

"Oh my, have y'all seen the latest post?" Ava fanned her face with her hand.

"Uh, what?" Becca asked.

24

Sawyer and Lena cracked up. The girls were at one end while the guys sat at the other talking sports and other guy stuff. "She's referring to her favorite site now," Lena replied.

"Yeah, Becca you've got to check this out. It's crazy good, at the very least entertaining to read." Sawyer snorted as she pulled it up on her phone. "Cowgirl Crazy is the talk of the town. Nobody knows who the site belongs to, but it's been rumored this chick is local."

"You don't say." Becca looked around the room and took a huge sip of her beer. "I-I'll have to check it out sometime."

"There's no time like the present." Sawyer handed her the phone she held. "This Cowgirl Crazy girl, E, has some seriously good recs too. Tried some of the stuff listed, and let me tell you..." She blew out a big breath and rolled her eyes back.

"Your expression tells us everything." Lena laughed. "We really don't need the full details."

Ava giggled.

"Okay, enough of that, poor Becca here is as bright as a tomato." Sawyer took her phone back. It was better for everyone to think she was shy, instead of being detected as the "local chick" who'd created their favorite site. Although she felt flattered, she also needed a serious subject change, stat.

Somebody above must have heard her silent plea because Liam came to the rescue. "Hey, Ava, have you asked Sawyer about the tattoo we talked about yet?"

Thank God!

"I was getting to it." Ava turned to Sawyer. "Liam

and I were talking about getting matching tattoos. I'd like you to do mine considering the placement."

"And where might that be?" Sawyer lifted a brow.

"I was wanting a yellow rose with a barbed wire heart surrounding it on my butt," Ava said, "Liam was going to get Mace to circle the barbed wire around his upper arm with the yellow rose in the middle." She bit her lip.

"That works," Sawyer nodded, "Mace and I can do a few sketches for you both to check out. When I get back to the shop tomorrow, I'll give you a call. Let you know when you should stop by for a consult. You can both look at the designs we've come up with and let us know if you'd like any changes done to it, things like that. From there we can make an appointment for the permanent ink."

"Thank you, this is so exciting!" Ava clapped enthusiastically and they all chuckled.

"Ooh, Alex, maybe we should get something done too," Lena remarked.

"We'll see how you feel about that come morning sweetheart, and I'll keep it in mind," Alex said, looking skeptical.

"What'chya thinking about?" Mace whispered, and she jumped. Becca hadn't noticed him approach. He grabbed the empty chair beside her and sat close. She'd been vaguely listening in on the conversations around her, and distracted with thoughts about her other persona, and the site everyone seemed to love.

"I was thinking I might try that bull over there soon." She pointed in the direction of the cowboy currently riding it. "Caught my eye as soon as I walked in."

"Mm, now this I'd love to see." Mace smirked. "Think you can handle that?" He tipped his head towards the same cowboy who was now on the floor.

"Oh, I can ride." Becca winked. "Care to make a bet?"

"I like the way you think," he said, his eyes taking on a mischievous glint. "What do you have in mind?"

"Let's see." She steepled her fingers while in thought and tapped her chin. "If I win you have to wash my car, by hand." She could picture it now, Mace shirtless and full of suds. What a sight.

"Done, and if I win I get a kiss before the night's over." He smiled. "Now the terms of our bet?"

"We ride the bull!" she exclaimed, knowing this was about to get good. This situation was a win/win as far as she was concerned. "The first one to fall off is the loser."

"You're on, sexy." Mace stood. "Hey, Jagger I'm gonna need you for a minute."

It was set, after Mace explained their little wager to everyone they sat with, they mutually agreed Jagger would be timing them both.

Game on.

Becca rubbed her hands together and eyed the machine. It was ladies first of course, and she had a chorus of cheers from the sidelines. Let the battle of the sexes begin. She took a deep breath and mounted the mechanical beast. After securing her hand, she gave a nod to Liam to start it up.

One, two, three, weee!

She rocked back and forth with her free hand waving in the air. It bucked wild back and forth, round and round, and side to side, it was exhilarating.

27

Her ass slammed up and down, her curvy body lurched forward, and she slid to the side all the while trying to hold on for dear life. Then all too soon, her grip loosened and she landed on the padded floor.

Becca stood up and rubbed her butt.

"Way to go, Becca!" Sawyer yelled, and everyone else whistled and cheered. She instantly sought out Mace and got butterflies. His lust filled gaze never left her face as he closed the distance, and she licked her lips.

"Fuck, that was hot, but it's my turn now, sweetness. I can't wait to see if you taste as good as you look," he growled, and helped her off the mat. Mace took his position as she sidled up to Jagger.

"So how did I do?" she asked.

"Not too bad." Jagger kept it vague as he watched the clock and her opponent ride.

"You were great!" Sawyer wrapped an arm around her shoulders and gave her a squeeze. "It looks like so much fun. I'm next."

Becca chuckled, and Mace was on the floor now. "Well?" She turned to Jagger again.

Mace joined them. "How'd I do?"

"Sorry, man, Becca has you beat by a couple of seconds." Jagger shook his head, and she whooped with joy.

"Congrats, come on, Jag. It's my turn," Sawyer said, and the other couple walked off to get her situated.

"You ready to clean?" She teased. "There is nothing sexier than a man who knows how to do his chores. Did I mention I'm hoping you'll be shirtless too?"

"I think that can be arranged." He pulled her closer by her belt loops. "You got lucky honey."

"Truth be told, it's been awhile. But, you never know, Tattoos. I may get lucky one day soon." Flirting came naturally around this man and she was feeling bold.

"Just say the word." He groaned. "And I'd be happy to make that happen for you."

"I'll keep that in mind." Becca reached up and caressed the side of his face. "In the meantime, I think you should be rewarded for effort." Her hand moved to the back of his head and she encouraged him forward. Her fingers slid through his hair and stayed there through the kiss. Her lips met his and she took it slow to savor him. One peck turned into two before her tongue slid inside and met with his. Her soft curves pressed against his muscular frame and the moment was Heaven on Earth. She was so consumed, everything around them faded and it felt like they were the only two in the room. Mace's hands wrapped around her tighter, the heat of his touch ignited her butterflies of excitement. She was so wet, her pussy ached. She rubbed against him and he reached down to squeeze her ass. It was so good, and then the moment screeched to a halt the moment they heard someone clear their throat from beside them.

Becca pulled back and pressed her forehead against his chest to catch her breath.

"What?" Mace grumbled, and she looked over to see their group looking smug. Their friend Liam laughed. "As hot as that was for everyone to see I think it's time we get back to the party." The proprietor couple, Liam and Ava, ushered everyone back towards the table and raised their glasses for a toast. "To great friends, good times, and strong unions. Congratulations, Sawyer and Jagger, here is to many years of happiness together."

Everyone took a sip and congratulated the happy couple again. Mace draped an arm around Becca's shoulders and pulled her as close as possible, then it dawned on her. "Oh, I almost forgot." She palmed her forehead and went to search her purse. "Here's your key. Feel free to bring your baby over anytime."

"Thanks," he said, pocketing it. "Now, how about a dance?"

"She's With Me" by High Valley started playing on the jukebox, and she accepted the hand he offered her to escort them to the dance floor.

Now, this should be interesting.

"You've proven you've got moves tonight on that mechanical bull, now I'm gonna show you I've got the moves too." Mace winked at her. She started the dance in his arms, and before she knew it, they twirled, grinded, and two-stepped their way to a great time. It was a blast.

Brody Mace had skills there was no doubt about it, and she couldn't remember the last time she'd smiled and laughed so much in her life. It was a memory she wouldn't soon forget.

Chapter Three

Becca

The next day, she checked the comments again on her last post. Thankfully Lusty Cowboy aka 'creepy guy' had only left the one. She breathed a sigh of relief as she scrolled through to figure out her next sexy request, and this one caught her eye.

Committed but Curious wrote:

"It's so refreshing to be able to ask questions or make requests about something so intimate without being judged for it thanks to the anonymity this site provides us, thank you for that. I'm a huge fan of Cowgirl Crazy so here goes. My fiancé and I have been together for five years total. Seeing as we're in a long-term relationship, we'd like to spice things up a little. We've used a couple of your suggestions so far and it's been really good, but lately he's expressed an interest in anal, and we haven't done that before. I'm just wondering if you could recommend a good lube, and

31

maybe some toys we could use so I can practice a little before the real thing happens. I'll be crossing my fingers that out of all the requests you truly consider mine. Thanks again in advance, CBC."

Becca smiled, took a deep breath, and began to write her next post.

A Story to Tell,

Welcome back my crazy but loyal readers. Last week I truly found out how popular this place has become, and I am eternally grateful. I began this anonymous journey to escape what was my otherwise normal boring existence. As y'all know my romantic life has been in a rut for quite some time now, but things are looking up. Remember Mr. Tall, Tattooed, and Tempting? I'm happy to note we're making progress.

Speaking of...

I also recall my promise to tell you more about our first encounter. So here you have it.

Mr. Fantasy Man showed up out of nowhere and took my breath away. He was totally out of my league. I could hear the rumble of his bike in the distance and caught my first glimpse of the stranger as he pulled into the gas station across the way. He wore a dark helmet, form fitting jeans, boots, and worn leather. He was a delectable distraction from afar. Now tell me ladies, what is it that makes us gravitate towards the bad boys? As I was coming out of the post office on Cully, he'd just finished paying his bill and was on his way to the bike again when I got my first glimpse of his face. Whew! From there I was all thumbs and two left feet. I dropped my parcel, which by the way, was from one of my sponsors on this site so you can imagine my embarrassment when not only had Mr. Fantasy Man noticed but so had one of my older business colleagues down the street. I rushed to get everything together and out of sight, only I wasn't fast enough. The sexy stranger knelt to help me out, of course, noticing some of the toys I desperately tried to keep hidden. His easy smile didn't help ease my embarrassment. I was literally caught red-handed, yet he never mentioned the obvious to me, and he saved me further embarrassment by distracting the nosy old lady rushing toward us with good intentions mixed in. The man was kind of sweet, not such a bad boy after all. He properly introduced himself, as did I, and he led the old lady away as he promised to see me again sometime soon.

And, the rest is history.

Since then we've seen each other on occasion and have become friends with potential. He's unknowingly fueled my desire and has given me hope, so wish me luck with this. Before running into him I was about ready to swear off men in general...lol.

In the meantime, I've gone through the comments on last week's post, and I've decided to give a shout out to Committed but Curious. Your crossed fingers worked honey, let me test out a few of those products and I'll get back to y'all in a few days with some good recs for anal play.

Pleasurable encounters, and pleasant dreams,
Your number one Cowgirl Crazy lady,
E.
XO

***

Mace

Home, that's what the tattoo shop had become. The moment he had the needle in his hand, heard the buzz from around the room as it hit the skin of whoever was in his chair and he was in his element. It was peaceful while he was in the zone, a place where he could escape in his artwork and share it with others. Since he could barely get the sexy brunette realtor out of his head outside of work, it gave his aching nut sack a break too. Damn, but he needed to get laid and pronto. Although blue balls sucked, he had a feeling Becca would be worth the wait.

Right now, though, all that mattered was his client's happiness and the piece of art he was currently creating on her arm. He hummed to the background music and wiped her skin with a paper towel to clear the excess ink away.

"Hey, lover boy, we've got a two o'clock with Liam and Ava. You finished the sketches they asked for right?" Sawyer asked while looking over his shoulder.

"Finished last night." He grunted, dipped his needle in more ink, and grouched, "Knock it off with the lover boy shit."

His client giggled. "I don't know, Mace, I have a feeling the name precedes you." He lifted a brow curiously while the woman winked at him and then he shook his head.

Women go figure.

"Oh, it does." Sawyer giggled. "You should have seen him the other night at Tipsy's with Ms. Becca Everett." She wiggled her eyebrows up and down and pretended to fan herself.

"Pity." His client pouted and he could feel his face heat up. *Fuckin' Sawyer.* She was lucky he loved her like family.

"I think that's enough talk about me." Mace turned his head to look up at the pest he treated like a sister. "Beat it, squirt. I'm tryin' to work over here, unlike some people."

"Yeah, yeah, yeah." Sawyer chuckled and walked away with a smile.

"So, is it serious?" his client asked.

"Say what?" Mace stopped again and sat back.

"With the girl, Becca, because if it's not you and I could get to know each other better sometime…"

Shit, is this chick for real?

"Think so." He cleared his throat. "I appreciate the offer, but I'm content with my status the way it is."

"Right." She nodded. "Can't blame a girl for trying."

"I'll keep that in mind." He smiled right then, and instead of encouraging her he went back to it with the remainder of his session in blissful silence.

Twenty-five minutes later after explaining the aftercare instructions to his client, he was done with her and getting ready for his next appointment. Liam and Ava would be there in about fifteen, and he had a few words for Sawyer.

The pain in the ass sat in the front of the shop on the computer engrossed in whatever it was she was looking at. "You mind telling me what that was all about?" he asked while he pointed over his shoulder with his thumb in the direction of his station.

Sawyer snickered. "Relax, bro, saw the chick checking you out is all and figured I'd let her know what's what. I like Becca and I think she'd be good for you."

He snorted. "Well, for future reference you'd do good to know I can handle myself when it comes to the ladies."

"Suit yourself." Sawyer shrugged. "All forgiven?"

"Yeah," Mace said and ruffled her hair. It had the added effect of pissing her off, great payback for the earlier shit she pulled by putting him on the spot. It was just the two of them now, but not for long. Mad Ink had a pretty steady schedule of clientele.

"Ooh, she's going anal!" Sawyer squealed and clapped her hands.

What. The. Fuck?

"The hell you say?" he asked. "What kind of shit are you looking at over here?"

"Cowgirl Crazy, damn, Mace, you've got to check this site out." She laughed. "It's this local chick that writes about personal experiences, gives recommendations, and takes requests from busy, lonely likeminded women in town and from God only knows where else in the world. It's humble, educational, and crazy funny other times. Only nobody knows who she is. It's completely anonymous but all about sex."

"Are you serious?"

"As a heart attack, we're talking experiences, positions, stories, toys of the adult variety, and recommendations. She's a hit. Check these sponsors out." Sawyer got up and pushed Mace into the chair she vacated. It's frickin' awesome."

"And nobody has figured out who this chick could be?" he clarified as he began to read her latest post.

"Me and the girls have had a few guesses, but nothing concrete." She shrugged. "It'd be intriguing to find out, but otherwise meh, it's entertaining and she knows what she's talkin' about. I've tried some of those recommendations of hers and…"

"Stop yourself right there." He shuddered.

"Whatever," Sawyer said and shoved him in the shoulder. "What'd you think?"

"Give me a minute to finish," he grunted and tuned her out, so he could continue reading it.

Well fuck me! I knew my Angel had a naughty side. Becca, Becca, Becca…hmm.

It just had to be her, the gas station, the nosy neighbor, him helping her pick things up and leading the old lady away so she could compose herself from embarrassment. It was just good to know that she felt the same kind of pull that he had. Mace groaned as his dick got hard and he fidgeted in his seat to get more comfortable. Thank fuck, Sawyer had showed this to him because if the lovely Becca needed any help with her research he was just the guy to lend her a hand, or his cock for her personal use to explore at any time. Damn, but he needed to see her soon, and not because of what he'd just read, although he liked it a whole heck of a lot.

He missed her.

So, it was time to do something about it. Tonight after work was said and done he'd finally bring his car over to store in the barn and settle his debt for the bet he made with her and then lost. She rode the hell out of that bull the other night at the bar and he owed her a car wash for it.

"Well?" Sawyer patiently waited for him to say something about it.

"Just like you said, interesting." Mace smiled because she looked disappointed and that was all the opinion she was going to get out of him. He was a man for fuck's sake. She wanted conversation she needed to talk to someone else about it. He was also going to keep the whole Becca assumption to himself.

The thought of talking more about the sex website with someone he considered a sister had the desired effect of deflating his chubby. Just in time too because Liam and Ava walked through the door at that very moment and it was time to show them some designs and ink some skin once again. He loved his job and his life.

Everything was looking up.

***

Lusty Cowboy

There was a fine line between love and hate, and

as he sat there in front of his computer screen reading Becca's latest post he could feel his anger simmer to a boiling point. He'd been eyeing her for a while now before he'd put two and two together that she was in fact his fantasy woman, Cowgirl Crazy's, E. He'd figured it out from her "Curious Minds" post. He was born and raised in Kerrville and had only known one woman whose parents had died, leaving her to raise her brother on her own. One woman who was also career driven and often alone. He was sure it was her. It had to be.

A complete lady with a naughty side equaled instant love in his eyes, unlike the last bitch who had broken his heart.

There was only one woman in his life now and she didn't really count. What he wanted, no needed, was a romantic interest, his Becca. Only now she talked about some tattooed guy like he was Heaven on Earth, and he couldn't allow it to continue for much longer.

"Argh!" he screamed and threw his coffee cup across the room. The hot liquid sprayed and the mug shattered on impact once it hit the basement wall. "Soon my sweet, Becca, I'll be seeing you very, very soon my love."

He growled now, and decided to leave a comment under his alias, Lusty Cowboy once again:

"Not anonymous to me anymore, I've figured it out and I'd love to fulfill that desire you speak of. Your pleasurable encounters are in my fantasies and you'll definitely be in my dreams, my naughty girl. See you soon. ~LC~"

"Now that should do it." He chuckled while talking to himself. In the meantime, he had plans to make.

"Baxter Bane Coulter, what are you doing down there? I heard a crash."

"Nothing, Grams, I dropped something. I'll be right up." He could hear the nosy old lady grumble from upstairs before she shut the door, and he hit send. At least now she'd know he was thinking about her and he couldn't wait before he permanently made her his to keep. It was only a matter of time, and a little bit of patience. No other man was going to take that away from him. He'd make sure of it.

***

Becca

Oh, what a day.

Her hands were full. She juggled her bag and the groceries she'd picked up for dinner, as she fished for her keys to unlock the door while trying not to drop anything. Her throat was so dry she was spitting cotton, and the Texas heat was so hot today the hens were laying hard boiled eggs. Sweat trickled from her forehead and laid a trail right down her cleavage. Becca couldn't wait to get out of these work clothes and into something more comfortable. She'd been on her feet the entire day, showing a few properties to a nice but indecisive newly married couple just starting out. And, she'd gotten another creepy message from Lusty Cowboy on the site.

She shivered. It was good to be finally home.

"Oomph!" To top it all off she just tripped over her own two feet as soon as she got the door open and landed flat on her face. It couldn't get any worse, or at least she hoped. "Ugh, here we go," she mumbled and began to pick up her mess.

Thirty minutes later, she was showered, dressed in shorts and a tank, the groceries were put away, and she was enjoying a nice glass of sweet tea.

The rumble of a muscle car close by caught her attention and she hurried to the window to see it. She smiled wide as soon as she noticed Mace behind the wheel, and damn, his toys were just as badass as the man himself. She loved the Harley, but this—this car was a beautiful piece of history. Old as dirt, but a classic none the less and she could appreciate that. She hadn't known much about his Yenko as he called it, but she could appreciate its solid body, the shiny red paint job, and sleek chrome. The engine revved as he drove around to the back of the house where the barn was located, and she figured she'd meet him outside and offer him a drink since it was so hot and all. It was not only her duty as a good hostess, but an excuse to talk to him again. It was good to see him.

She grabbed a glass, filled it with ice, poured some tea, and garnished it with a lemon wedge before she escaped out the back door.

He just finished exiting the car when she walked inside. The car fit perfectly in the space they'd cleared, and she was glad Mace seemed to like it for the time being. He noticed her immediately, so she held the glass out to him. "I thought you might like this." Becca handed it to him and traced her fingers across the body of the car as she admired it up close.

41

"You like it?"

"Do I?" she said and nodded yes. "I had no idea what you were talking about when you mentioned your baby, but this—this is really nice, Mace. Will you take me for a ride sometime?"

"You just say the word, babe, and I'll give you a ride any damn time you'd like." He smirked, and she blushed, noting the double entendre.

She cleared her throat. "Tell me about it."

"What the car or the ride?" He chuckled. "It's a '68 Camaro Yenko, the Holy Grail for any Chevy enthusiast. They only made about a couple hundred of these babies. It's got a 425-horse power 427 big block under the hood and rides like a dream. My pop gave it to me before he died going on six years now and I've been fixing her up for a while. Once I'm done she'll be worth a mint, but I won't be selling so it doesn't matter anyway." He shrugged and began to chug the drink she offered.

"I'm sorry for your loss, Mace. I can see why the car means a lot to you now." She moved closer and squeezed his arm in a show of support.

He reached up to tuck a stray hair behind her ear that escaped from her messy bun and changed the subject. "Speaking of cars, I seem to recall a sexy woman out riding me on a mechanical bull the other night." He groaned, "It was hot, by the way, and I am now tasked with washing her car."

"You really don't have to," she said trying to brush it off, but she could see he wasn't having it. Mace arched his left eyebrow and shook his head.

"But I do, babe. I'm a man of my word." He lowered his face and planted a quick kiss on her lips before stepping back again. "And if I recall the request was for it to be shirtless." He didn't wait for her answer before he fisted the back of his shirt in his hand and pulled it over his head.

Holy sweet mother of...

She was utterly speechless. Smooth skin, hard muscle, rippling abs, and ink as far as the eye could see, oh my.

He hooked a finger under her chin to close her mouth and winked. "Now, how about you show me where the supplies are."

"Follow me," she said and led the way.

She gathered a bucket, the hose, soap, and sponges, and decided to help so it would go faster. "Do you have any plans after we're done here?" she asked while she lathered soap on the hood.

"Not really," he said. "Do you have anything in mind?"

"How about dinner?" She suggested, "I've got some steak we could throw on the grill, if you're interested."

"Sounds good to me," he agreed and then turned on the hose to rinse the side he was working on.

"Oh no you didn't!" Becca squealed. As Mace washed the soap off, the water also sprayed in her direction and it was cold. Her nipples pebbled, and she shivered from the unexpected spray headed in her direction.

Mace guffawed. "Wet looks really good on you."

"It does, does it?" She teased and raced around to meet him. He playfully held her back as she tried to wrestle the hose away from him. He gave in after a few minutes and ran as she gained control of it to get him back.

He somehow managed to creep up behind her and laughed as she squeaked in surprise while also dropping the hose to the ground the moment he had his arms around her. She loved the sound of his laughter but loved it even more the minute he turned her around, so he could kiss her again. It was better than she remembered too. His lips were so soft and plump as they pressed against her own. It started off slowly at first, but the moment their tongues touched an inferno ignited and she was on fire for him. They weren't playing anymore. Mace lifted her off her feet and backed them up until her butt rested on top of the hood. Her legs spread for him, so he could get as close as possible and he squeezed her hips with his fingers. She could feel the hard ridge of his cock through his jeans and rubbed her wet core against it. She moaned and her chest heaved as her breathing sped up. Her hips thrust against him, dry humping and it felt so good.

"Oh, Mace…" Becca arched her back to push her breasts against his chest. His lips trailed across her jaw and down her neck.

"That's it, baby," He growled, "Will you come for me?"

"Please…" Was all she managed to whimper. She'd made herself come millions of times, but it had been so long since she'd had a man's touch and it was bliss.

He flicked the button on her jean shorts open and slid his hand inside her damp panties. She was so wet for him, and it had nothing to do with their water fight. Warm and wanting, it wouldn't take long. His fingers skimmed through her slippery folds and circled her engorged clit, applying just enough pressure to make her crazy. Her breath hitched, and she held onto his arms tightly as he played her like a finely tuned instrument.

"That's it, baby. Give it me. You're so fucking beautiful, and breathtaking, Becca."

Her whole body shook and she lost control. "H-holy shitttt, Mace, yes, YES!" His mouth consumed her cries of ecstasy, kissing her senseless until she found calm again. He slowed everything down after a few minutes more and pulled back. His breathing was still heavy as he pressed his forehead against hers to gain his own composure.

"That was, um, that was…"

"Wow." He finished her sentence and shook his head as if he was in disbelief. "What you do to me."

"Ditto." Becca returned. Mace backed away just enough to help her put her feet back on the ground.

"Here's the plan. I'm going to need a minute to calm down, so I can finish with this car and then join you for dinner before I forget where we are again and take you right here and now. You deserve better than that." He smiled at her, but it looked more like a grimace. Before he could continue, she did.

"And, while that happens I'll go in, change my clothes, and get dinner started. Will you be okay out here?"

"Yeah, babe, totally worth it." He lifted her hand to his lips. "See you in a few."

"Looking forward to it." Becca gulped as she turned around to head inside. There were so many emotions swirling around inside of her that she had so long ago suppressed, and she was falling hard for Mace. It was both exhilarating and scary all at once. Yet as she thought about it she knew without a doubt he would be worth the risk to her heart. She just needed to take it one day at a time.

Chapter Four

Mace

Earlier had been a big tease.

They'd just finished eating dinner, her car was sparkling clean, and he was still trying to figure out a way to approach the subject of Cowgirl Crazy. He couldn't get it out of his head. One, she needed to know that he obviously was just as into her as she seemed to be into him. Two, he was proud of her and all that she had accomplished. It was quite the blog. Yet, he could already tell that whatever Becca did she dedicated one hundred ten percent to. Her home, the buildings she owned and leased, as well as her realty business were a testament to that. She was quite successful. That, and sexy, sweet, and she smelled good too, his kind of woman. The list went on.

Then an idea hit, and it started off with leaving a few words, short and sweet.

Mace leaned back against the couch as Becca went to put his clothes in the dryer and then said she was going to prepare some coffee for them both. She'd lent him a pair of jogging pants and a Tee that belonged to her brother. They were a bit snug, but it was better than sticking around in wet clothes thanks to their water fight. He pulled out his phone and pulled up the site. After signing in he decided to go with the name she had given him as his username, *Tattoos,* and he began typing.

Tattoos wrote:

"I remember that very day like it was yesterday. Loving those nicknames by the way. And, it's nice to also know you feel the same way I do. Your secrets are safe with me. XOXO Tattoos, aka. Tall, Tempting, and Tattooed, or shall I go with Mr. Fantasy Man? *Wink*"

"What are you up to?" Becca smiled as she handed him a mug of coffee. She joined him on the sofa and got comfortable. He left his phone on and turned a bit, so he could face her.

Here goes nothing.

"Earlier at work Sawyer showed me something interesting," he said, and then scooched closer to the middle so he could sit next to her.

"Really?" Becca bit her lip. "Sawyer's a blast, so I can just imagine what it was."

"She's something all right." Mace placed his cup on the table beside him, and then reached for her cup to do the same. He took one hand from her lap and held it. "Remind me to thank her later for showing it to me. Right now, though, I'd much rather concentrate on another amazing woman. You see,

48

thanks to her I was introduced to a unique website, an informative one, one that's clearly personal yet helps so many others. Have you heard of it?"

Mace could pinpoint the exact moment Becca figured it out. Her mouth dropped open and then closed as if she wanted to say something but was at a loss for words, the color seemed to drop from her face, and she cleared her throat after avoiding his eye contact. Suddenly the floor was much more interesting than he was, and he couldn't have that now, could he?

He nudged her chin with his finger, so she could look at him again, and she seemed to compose herself just a little better. "H-heard of what?" she stuttered.

"It's called Cowgirl Crazy, but I think you already know that." He prompted softly. "Here..." He handed her his cell to look at. "I'd like you to read this."

She reluctantly nodded, and began to read the last comment posted, his. It only took a few seconds and her hands shook as she handed it back. He steadied them as he took her hands inside of his again and held them still. "I promise I won't say anything if you'd still like to keep your anonymity. I just wanted you to know I felt the same way about you. Honestly, it was just a fluke that I happened to read the post of how we met when I did. I'm flattered, and I swear no one knows anything, not from me anyway."

A single tear fell down her cheek. She wiped it away quickly and took a deep breath. "Okay." She continued with a couple more deep breaths to calm herself some and then tried her best to relax.

"This is so embarrassing," she said and laughed

without humor. "I clearly need to be more careful."

"You should, but I also think you should be proud." He said, "You're clearly helping others on it. People look up to you, they relate to you, admire you even. It's also hot as Hell." He winked, and she blushed again. He'd never get tired of that. Mace placed their entwined hands over his heart. "I mean it, Becca. You've got a gift here at whatever you do in life and if you can't acknowledge that, I'm prepared to be proud enough for the both of us." He pulled her forward slightly, so he could place a kiss on her forehead. "You get me?"

"Got it," she whispered, "just please don't say anything. I'm not ready for everybody to know who I am."

"My lips are sealed. Trust me."

"Thank you," she said, and she seemed relieved now, so he smiled, especially when she threw her arms around his neck and began kissing him hungrily.

Body language was his favorite type of communication. She climbed on his lap and he leaned back so he could give her more room to explore. There was no issue as far as he was concerned with allowing her to lead this as far as she wanted too. His blood headed south to his cock and it ached to be set free.

"So, then I guess you saw my latest request?" Becca whispered while trying to catch her breath.

Is she talking about…? Shit I hope so.

"You mean with the curious girl, right?" Mace wanted to tread carefully to make sure he wasn't reading into this wrongly. The last thing he needed was to come across as an ass, so he had to have her spell it out for him.

"That's the one." Becca said, and she tilted her head sideways as she studied his reaction. "She's interested in anal play with her long-term lover and I was hoping to help her out with that. Lube education is important in that situation, and I figured I could suggest a toy or two, so I was rummaging around my toy box earlier and found a plug I could use and leave a review of, as well as a special silicone lube, Anal Ease. It's made specifically for this type of play and has a desensitizing agent for a more pleasurable encounter for the person receiving penetration. Care to be daring with me?"

"Please tell me you're serious." Mace moaned and thrust his hips upwards, so she could feel exactly how hard he'd become. He quickly got up from the couch and carried her with him. "Bedroom, babe, where is it?"

"Up the stairs, end of the hall." Becca chuckled.

He quickly followed her directions. They made their way upstairs safely and he devoured her mouth against his while he carried her down the hallway. Her hands fisted his hair and he pressed her against the wall while he fumbled to get her bedroom door open. He needed her naked, and pronto. He hadn't even been inside her yet and he could already tell she was something special. It was pure craziness and he had to fight not to come in his pants like some inexperienced teenager. He had a confident woman in front of him with a kinky need to explore. This had better not be a dream.

He walked them to her bed and squeezed her ass

before he let go. Becca bounced a couple of times and giggled.

She got onto her knees and pointed her index finger up. "Hold on to that thought. Let me just grab what we need." She winked and then crawled towards her nightstand. His gaze zeroed in on her ass and he licked his lips. A minute later she was standing in front of him and she yanked her top off.

"I love that you're so fuckin' eager." He growled, "I need to taste you."

Mace quickly flicked her bra loose and took it off so that her top half was bared to his gaze. Next, he undid the button on her shorts, and hooked his fingers along her underwear line. In one smooth motion he took both her panties and shorts and pulled them down. He threw them behind him not bothering to look where they landed. "You're so beautiful."

He kissed his way across her jaw and nibbled on her ear before his lips landed on her neck. His hands cupped her plump breasts, just a perfect size to fit inside of his hands. He caressed them and dragged his thumbs across her nipples. They pebbled for him, and she shivered. He replaced his fingers with his mouth this time, and she bowed to push her chest out, so she could get better access to his mouth there. Her bosom heaved with excitement, and she held the back of his head while he feasted on her.

"Mace, please," she whimpered, and he wanted to give her so much more.

He untangled himself from her embrace and licked his lips as he gently guided her to lie down on the bed behind.

"You're still overdressed," she said, leaning on

her elbows. He pulled the shirt off his back, but his pants remained.

"Is that better?"

"But you're still…" She pouted, but Mace interrupted her.

"Shh, we'll get there but until then my pants have to stay on." He needed the barrier between them for what he wanted to do next because the moment his dick sprang free he'd want to be balls deep inside her, and he wasn't finished tasting. Mace lifted her feet and kissed his way first down one leg and then the other. She moaned as he took his time doing it. He licked from her knee to her core and stopped just a breath away to admire her for a second before he continued. Becca gasped, and writhed for him, pushing her glistening pink cunt closer and he couldn't resist any longer. She was his new favorite flavor. They moaned in unison the moment he tongued her sweet spot and lapped her up. He explored her folds and sucked at her juices. She spread her fingers through his hair and tugged to place him where she needed him most. Mace chuckled as he obliged her silent request. His tongue circled her clit, up and down, round and round. Over and over again, he licked, flicked, and fucked her with his mouth. Her body began to shake, and her moans became louder. She was close, and it was such a turn on to see and hear.

That's it, baby, come.

He thought it, and she exploded for him. She writhed, moaned, and shouted out his name while he kept licking and drinking her in. He stood the moment she stilled and yanked down his pants. His cock sprang forward, saluting proudly and he quickly reached over for the condom Becca had left at the foot of the bed. He slipped it on and crawled on top of her.

"I need to be inside of you so badly," he said, but despite his words and his eagerness to do just as he'd said he didn't rush to it.

Mace tucked some hair behind her ear and kissed her tenderly as she spread her legs wider to welcome him. It was all the invitation he needed, and he entered her in one smooth stroke to the hilt.

"Shit, Becca." He groaned, "You're so tight baby, so good." He thrust slowly to try and prolong their pleasure.

It was utter bliss.

***

Becca

"Mace wait," Becca bit her lip and pushed against his chest. As much as she loved having him fuck her traditionally she still needed him in other ways.

There was time for traditional later.

Mace grimaced, but he immediately stopped his thrusting. "What's the matter?"

"Nothing, really, I'm loving this—us together, but…" She reached above her head to grab the box of lube and held it between them. "I was wondering if we could finish this, anal."

"You're too good to be true, I swear." She could feel him swell inside of her as if the thought of having her in the ass made him even harder. He pulled out eagerly, took the lube from her grasp and began to open the box. As he stood in front of the bed she had her first opportunity to check him out thoroughly, and he was magnificent. Thick broad shoulders, muscular pecks, and six pack abs. His chest had a little bit of hair down to the treasure trail leading to his cock. She licked her lips as she admired his V to the shaft that stood out. He was thick, and long, the condom still on him wet with her juices. He had the lube open now, poured some in his hand and she cursed the moment he gripped himself. He began stroking the lube on his condom covered cock from root to tip. It was a sexy sight.

Mace smirked at her as she watched him. "Don't want this to hurt for you babe," he grunted. Once his dick was full of lube, he squirted more from the bottle onto his index and middle finger. He threw the bottle on the side of the bed and softly approached her. "You want this missionary, or would you like to be on all fours for this?"

Becca bit her lip as she thought about it, also touched that he had asked. Her heart beat faster, and it swelled as she thought of how much care he was giving her. He must have been aching for a release. "Like this," she whispered, deciding on the missionary route so that she could look into his eyes as he loved her. So, she could also kiss him, and touch him whenever she felt the need too.

"Okay then, spread 'em baby." Mace crawled onto the bed in front of her and pushed her legs a little wider. She startled the moment his fingers slid through her ass crack and the cold lube met her puckered hole. He was gentle when he rubbed some of the silicone gel around it. He began to finger her. He started with one finger and followed it by a second. It took a few minutes to get used to, and the penetration burned slightly before it got better. Soon enough though she began to feel an amazing sensation throughout her entire body and she was matching his finger thrusts with thrusts of her own.

"I think someone's ready," Mace growled.

"God, yes." Becca moaned. There was hunger written all over his face that she was sure was also in her own gaze.

The tip of his cock slowly entered her, and she encouraged him to completely fill her by pushing herself down on it until he was fully sheathed. "I. Need. You."

"Heck, yeah you do," he said, and pumped into her faster. Her breast bounced, her nipples hardened, she was being fucked thoroughly just the way she wanted, how she wanted it, and her whole body was overcome with pleasure. It was a sensational experience all around.

He gave her a quick kiss on the lips before he dragged her legs with him to the edge of the bed. Mace slowly stood while still connected to her, and he held her legs while he continued to pump into her faster. "I'm gonna come soon. Come. With. Me." He stroked her clit, which only heightened the experience tenfold, and it only took a moment for her to shatter. She pulsed, and quaked while he filled the condom inside of her with his own orgasmic bliss.

Her chest heaved, and they were both slick with sweat by the time Mace collapsed on top of her to catch his breath. Becca stroked his back and giggled.

"Wow!"

"You could say that again." Mace leaned on his elbows and kissed her. "Give me an hour and I'll probably be ready for the next round."

"Are you serious?" She looked at him wide eyed. "I'm impressed."

"You haven't seen anything yet. Just let me get rid of this and I'll be right back." He got up, winked at her and pointed to his crotch before walking out of the room in search of the bathroom. He needed to dispose of the used condom.

True to his word he was ready to go again in half of the time he estimated, and it got better and better. They hadn't used the small butt plug she'd brought out originally, so it was put to good use the second time around. Mace filled her up, and double penetrated her with the toy she needed to review for Committed but Curious. It had been so long since she'd had the real thing and it was far better than she remembered it could be. Thanks to Mace she had completely and irrevocably come undone. We were talking head over heels in love. Was there such a thing as love at first sight? Because looking back she knew that's exactly what happened, and it was a little scary giving your heart to a man who knew you liked him, claimed he liked you back. He just didn't know the depth of it.

Chapter Five

Becca

Early rays of sunshine shone through a crack in her curtains. Becca squinted and stretched her entire body. She was a little sore, but completely satisfied. She smiled, closed her eyes again, thought of the previous night's mattress gymnastics, and rolled over to give Mace a good morning kiss. But, he wasn't beside her. Instead he sat at the edge of the bed completely engrossed in his own thoughts. Acoustic musical notes sounded around the room, and it surprised her to hear them coming from the normally mounted guitar she had displayed in the corner of the room. It was once her father's and she hadn't heard it played since she was a teen, right before the car accident happened.

He must have felt her gaze on him, because suddenly he stopped playing and turned his head her way to acknowledge her. "Morning, beautiful."

"Hey." She sat up and crawled to him. "Would

you play something for me?"

Mace obliged. While Becca listened she also took the opportunity to admire his tattoos. He was shirtless, so she took advantage and traced the large angel that took the expanse of his back from shoulders to butt and then pressed soft kisses against it. One peck, two, three, and four, she then wrapped her arms around him and watched him from over his shoulder. "Have you been playing for long?"

"I picked it up in high school." He shrugged. "Haven't played for a while though." He tapped her arms to let go and got up to put the guitar where he found it. "How long ago did you learn guitar?"

"I haven't," she replied and smiled shyly. "It was my dad's once."

"I'm sorry," he said.

"Don't worry about it. You're really good."

"I'm good at a lot of things." Mace smirked and headed straight for her. He stood in front of the bed again and traced a finger down the side of her face. "Would you like another demonstration sweetheart?"

"How can I refuse?" She teased and went up to her knees. "How about we start with a kiss and then maybe you can catch up to me. Seeing as I'm already naked."

"So sexy," he growled, "and all mine." He framed her face with his hands and devoured her mouth. She leaned back on the bed, took him down with her, and loved every moment of their time together. Becca rolled over so that she was on top then she broke the kiss and went straight for his boxer briefs to yank them off.

"If I'm yours, does this mean this is all mine?" she

questioned, and grabbed his dick by the base as soon as his underwear came off.

"Anytime you want it babe," he groaned at the end of that sentence because he was at a loss for words the minute she licked around the head. Her hand pumped him, and she took him fully into her mouth. She sucked, and licked, bobbing her head all the way down until she hit her gag reflex. She relaxed her throat and Mace held her hair back, so he could watch her work him over and over. It was so erotic, powerful even to be in control this way, to please him.

His breathing was labored, and he cursed. He must have been close to completion. "Becca," he called. "Becca, baby?" He yanked on her hair to get her attention, but she was really into it. She didn't want to stop or slow down. Not unless he right out said so. He surprised her by sitting up and her mouth slid off him. She pouted, and he chuckled.

"That feels unbelievably good, trust me. I'd just rather finish like this." Becca squealed as he grabbed her ankles and flipped her over so that she now was not only on top, but her pussy straddled his face.

Hell yeah!

Mace was magic.

She grabbed his dick again and licked him like a big ol' lollipop from root to tip, only this time she was even more motivated to suck him off. His mouth latched onto her cunt like he was starving and in need of some serious sustenance. She worked him faster and ground herself against his face. The man really knew what he was doing to her. She wanted to return the favor. He played her body like a pro.

"Shit, Becca, I'm about to come so you might want to back off if you don't want to swallow me." He thrust his hips to fuck her mouth, and she thought it was really sweet he cared enough to warn her. Only she really wanted to go all the way, to taste him and savor the moment so she gripped him tighter, pumped him faster, and deep throated to the best of her ability to bring him there. His tongue lapped at her faster, he sucked her juices, licked her clit like nobody's business, and with a busy mouth full of pussy, he moaned once he let go. His cock pulsed jet streams of come down her throat, and she didn't stop until he was licked cleaned.

Becca collapsed her head on his leg and tried to catch her breath. She was close herself, so excited and completely at his mercy. "I think I'm in love with that mouth. Oh God, Mace, it's so incredible. I'm going to gush baby. Make. Me. Gush!" she hollered. At that moment she had reached her peak into oblivion.

She saw stars and it took her a moment to regain her equilibrium.

Mace rolled her over and she switched her position around so that he could hold her. She kissed him quickly and he smiled. "I love it when you talk dirty."

"Mm, I'll try to remember that. If only every morning could start off this well," she said.

"Where have you been all of my life?" He joked. "Do you have any plans for today?"

It was the weekend, a beautiful Saturday morning and after the hectic work day she had yesterday, she had two glorious days to herself, and for once in her life she planned to enjoy every moment of the free time ahead. "Nothing really, do you have something in mind?"

He shrugged. "I don't have to go into the shop today. Thought I could spend more time with you. Wherever you want to go, whatever you want to do."

Instead of answering right away, she climbed on top of him again and nipped his bottom lip. "I'd love to, Mace."

"You drive me crazy." He chuckled. "The good kind, my insatiable beauty."

"Likewise," she breathed. Her voice hitched the moment he caressed her breasts but before they could go any further the doorbell rang. "Damn, to be continued."

"You can count on it," he agreed.

Becca got up in search of her clothes. The doorbell rang again, and she hurried to get dressed to answer it, whoever it may be. She wasn't expecting anyone.

After racing down the stairs she took a deep breath, straightened her shirt and opened it.

"Bax?"

"Becca. You're looking beautiful," Baxter replied.

She looked down at herself and blushed. She was far from looking her best seeing as how she just got out of bed and all and was wishing she was still in it. She cleared her throat and gripped the door. "This is unexpected. How can I help you today?"

"Oh, uh, Grams sent me over to ask if you can give this to the committee Monday afternoon. It's the plans you all are supposed to take a vote on. I think it's for the theme for the next exhibit." He handed over a thick envelope and rocked back on his heels.

Becca was on the chair with Mrs. Coulter for the KACC for the last two years now and it wasn't like the old lady to miss out. "Is everything all right? She's not normally one to skip out on a meeting."

"She should be eventually. She's just been not feeling too well the last couple of days is all," he said and fingered the collar of his shirt. "It sure is a warm one out here. Feel like some company? I could sure use a drink."

"I think I have that covered," Mace said from behind her. Becca startled, she hadn't heard him approach and Baxter straightened his posture. "But I'm sure our sweet Becca has a bottle of water she can spare. Hang on a sec and I'll get that for you." Mace pulled her belt loop to bring her closer to him, turned her around and marked her with a kiss. She was left speechless for a moment as he took off down the hallway toward the kitchen.

"Um, I'm sorry about that," she mumbled, wasn't used to being involved in public displays of affection. Not that she was complaining. Mrs. Coulter had been hinting about her available grandson for a while now, but she hadn't been interested. Bax may have been interested enough for them both, but there had just been something about the guy that was off-putting. It was an instinct she couldn't shake. Hopefully this was the time he realized it just wasn't going to happen between them. "Mace and I have already made plans. I do hope your Grams gets well soon, and I'll be sure to keep her posted." She held up the envelope he'd given her and then set it on the table near the entryway. "I'll do my best to stop by in a day or two to check how she's doing and keep her in the loop."

"Yes well, she'll like that I'm sure," he replied, looking all kinds of uncomfortable as Mace once again approached.

"Here you go, man," Mace said and handed the beverage over. He draped an arm around her shoulders and pulled her in close to his side. Truth be told, she loved being there and hadn't minded that he'd staked his claim in front of Bax. Again, there was just something about the old lady's grandson that wasn't quite right. She just hadn't figured out what it was.

"Right, y'all have a good day then. I'll see you around, Becca. Count on it."

She shivered, and Mace shut the door.

"You okay?" he asked and looked her over from head to toe as of to make sure.

She nodded. "I'm just glad you're here."

"Me too," Mace grunted when she hugged him. "That guy is totally into you, you know that right?"

"Figured it out the moment Mrs. Coulter tried to set us up," she said into his chest. "Not interested."

"Good to know." He chuckled. "Who are you interested in?"

"Like you even have to ask, especially after last night and this morning." She snickered. "Loved the way you staked a claim with the kiss and the arm around me by the way."

"Is that so?" Mace snorted. "Think he took the hint?"

"He'd be a fool not to," she replied. "Now enough

64

about him and let's concentrate on us. I've worked up an appetite."

Becca pulled Mace with her toward the kitchen again. "I'll get breakfast started, you can make the coffee, and if you behave I'll let you wash my back in the shower when we're done."

"I love the way you think," Mace replied, and he smacked her ass when she turned around.

"Hey." She laughed. "You're supposed to behave."

"Couldn't help it." He winked. "You've got me addicted to touching you."

"The feeling's mutual big guy, now let's eat. I have a feeling I'll need the energy."

***

Becca

Kerrville was great for the many tranquil escapes along the beautiful Texas Hill Country, and she wanted to share some of them with Mace. There were many parks and water activities along the Guadalupe River and it seemed like something they both might enjoy.

"So where are we going?" Mace asked. He suggested she choose their outing today because he'd only been in town for a few months now, and he wasn't all that familiar with the attractions yet. Besides Tipsy's Bar, Mad Ink, Jagger's place, and Sawyers homestead where he was currently staying and fixing up, he hadn't really seen much else. Becca had been purposely tight lipped about it so far, so she could watch his reaction when they arrived.

"You'll see." She smirked. All he knew was that she'd packed them a picnic lunch, a blanket, and plenty of water to drink.

"Come on, just a hint?" he asked, and she sighed, giving in.

"I'm taking you to a park along the Guadalupe. It's one of my favorite spots. I figured we could eat lunch, swim a little, and do some hiking if you're up to it." She shrugged. She was currently driving and had to keep her eyes on the road, but she could still make out his smile from the corner of her eye. "The scenery is just so breathtaking. You're going to love it."

"It already is, Becca," he said.

"What already is?" She was confused. They were almost there, but he hadn't seen anything yet.

"You, my scenery, it's already beautiful." Mace stroked the side of her face, and chuckled when she shivered with goose bumps.

"Flattery will get you everywhere, Tattoos." She teased. "Keep it up and I may have to reward you again."

"Can't wait." He grinned.

"The feeling's mutual." Becca licked her lips and turned her blinker on. They'd finally arrived. "We're here."

They got out and Mace helped her with the backpack of supplies for the day. He put it on. Their lunch, water, a blanket, and some towels were stashed inside of it. Becca led him down a trail and figured they'd start with their hike first, where they would eventually find a spot by the river to eat and swim. Somewhere a little secluded and peaceful, she hoped.

"If we hike far enough along this trail, you'll be able to see an overlook of the river. Some of these trails are also open to horseback riders. You ever ride before?" she asked as Mace helped her over a rock.

"Only on my motorcycle," he said, winking at her. "And, that mechanical bull that one time."

"I remember that night fondly," she replied. "It was the first time you really kissed me."

"Not the first time I wanted to though."

She smiled at him. They held hands along the trail, and they could hear the water in the distance. She pointed a few things out along the way, and they both bird watched until they reached the overlook and decided that was as good a place as any to eat their lunch. Becca had packed them some leftover salad from the night before and made some steak sandwiches.

Mace laid the blanket she packed on the grass and helped himself to the food. They were both quiet while they ate but it was a peaceful silence, so it was nice.

"I'm glad you brought me here. It's not every day a man finds a woman who doesn't mind the outdoors," he said. "You continue to surprise me the more I get to know you. It's refreshing. I haven't met a woman quite like you before."

"Uh, thanks I think." Becca blushed. "What type of woman are you used to, then?" They were done eating now, and they both began to put away their food containers. Meanwhile, Mace took a moment to think about his answer.

"I came from a city much busier than what you're used to here, and truthfully I didn't really have a type until recently." He got up and handed her a bottle of water before they continued their hike to lower ground, so they could pick a spot to swim. "If I wasn't working, I had family obligations, and in the spare time that I managed to scrounge up to go out with anyone it was mostly a string of one-night stands that didn't mean anything."

"I understand," she said.

"Do you really?" Mace asked. "Until you I haven't ever wanted anything more than one night. You're different for me, and it blows my mind, but not enough to scare me away. I like you Becca, a hell of a lot."

"I like you too." She smiled and reached out to hold his hand again. "Probably more than I should considering the amount of time we've known each other."

"Exactly," he agreed. "But here we are."

"Here we are." She repeated. "I take it you no longer have the same family obligations now. Is that why you wanted a change?"

"Something like that. Mom was sick and passed away last year so when Toby mentioned Sawyer needed some help down here, I jumped at the opportunity. I needed the change of scenery from the bad memories, and we were worried about Sawyer after Carly died, so it seemed like the right thing to do." He explained. "Glad I did, cause I got to meet you."

"How are you not snatched up yet?" Becca shook her head in disbelief. "You intrigue me, and I haven't met anyone like you either."

"See we have so much in common." He teased.

She nodded in agreement and turned somber. "I'm sorry about your mom."

"Thank you," he whispered, and then stopped in his tracks. He traced a finger down her face and then tucked some hair behind her ear. "It was hard for a while, but I'm in a good place now. As for why I'm still single you asked?" He shrugged. "I hadn't met you yet, and now that I have I'm willing to negotiate that status with you if you're willing."

"How so?" She wondered. "It's been a while so you may have to spell it out for me."

"I love spending time with you, Becca, so I was hoping we could make this exclusive. I've never been in a relationship before, so I may screw up somehow. You may need to be patient with me at some point."

"I think I can manage that," she said. "Just so we're clear, are you asking me to be your girlfriend?"

"I guess I am," he replied.

"Exclusively?" she clarified.

"You're damn right." He growled, "No other men for you, and I haven't wanted another woman since the second I laid eyes on you."

"Yay!" She clapped, and Mace guffawed.

"So, is that a yes?"

"It's a yes!" she exclaimed. "A definite yes." Her heart swelled to maximum capacity she was so happy, and she jumped into his arms to kiss his whole face. "Now let's celebrate with a swim, and later I'll properly welcome you into boyfriend status."

Chapter Six

Becca

There's nothing like the real deal,
Hey y'all, here's another story to enjoy.

Once upon a time in the Hill Country of Texas there lived a grown woman who took a leap of faith. She'd been alone a long time and no longer believed in fairy tales, until recently. Only it wasn't Prince Charming who came to her rescue, he was somebody much better, more realistic. Rough, rugged, and gorgeous inside and out. His skin was a canvas of beautiful art, and he loved all things motorcycles and vintage muscle cars. He was a hardworking man who worked with his hands and made the world a more beautiful place to be, most especially mine.

That's right y'all, I'm a kept woman now and I want to share it with the world. Who needs the prince when you've got a man with tattoos, a big heart, and a big...

wink

He is the one and only Mr. Fantasy Man aka Mr. Tall, Tempting, and Tattooed I've been sharing about. After spending more time together we've realized we have a lot in common, and we just couldn't beat the chemistry that flows between us.

I'm so happy.

But, no worries I fully intend to keep the blog going so continue to ask me questions or send me requests. I'm here for y'all as always.

Now, it's back to business. The last time I wrote we talked about exploring anal play. Committed but Curious had written that she and her long-time partner were wanting to try it for the first time, and she requested my help on what she may be able to use to practice before the real thing. Well, I went through my rather big toy box and found some Crazy Girl Anal Ease. It's a silicone gel desensitizing lube meant to relax the anal muscles for a more pleasurable penetration experience. It's completely condom safe and is suitable for use with toys as well. Everyone has their own preferences, but I'd recommend going with a silicone-based lubricant instead of a water based one because it seems to last longer, it's thicker, and it makes for an easier glide inside. The Anal Ease gets five Cowgirl Crazy stars.

Now for some practice, if you're inexperienced in this area, I'd recommend using a small beginner-sized butt plug. They come in all sorts of shapes and sizes so if you enjoy the feeling you can eventually upgrade to something much larger. Always remember to use *plenty of lubricant though.*

Communication is always very important in a relationship. Remember to talk things through, especially when it comes to exploring sexually. Express your likes, dislikes, and concerns, always. Don't be shy. I hope this helps.

Don't forget to leave your comments. I'll be checking in every now and again and I'll choose our next adventure from them for next time.

Until then,

Pleasurable encounters, and pleasant dreams,

Your number one Cowgirl Crazy lady,

E.

XO

***

Mace settled into boyfriend status like a dream. A couple of weeks had gone by since their Guadalupe date, and they had spent every spare moment together ever since. She was running behind on some of her other obligations and decided to do a little catching up, starting with Mrs. Coulter.

The nosy but lovable old lady wasn't feeling well the last time Becca had called to keep her updated on the KACC exhibit. That was last week. She'd tried calling a few more times to check in on her again with no answer. So, she decided to drive over to see her in person instead. She'd told Bax she'd do that anyway.

Her cell rang and she turned on her Bluetooth to answer it.

"Howdy, Becca Everett speaking." She always answered in a formal way in case it was business related.

"Hello, beautiful." The deep timber of Mace's voice still made her heart beat a little faster, and the butterflies in her belly dance. "Miss you already."

"Well aren't you sweet." She smiled. "I took off work early because I'm fixin' to go see Ol' lady Coulter to check in."

"She still sick?" he asked with what sounded like a hint of worry, and she wondered if it was because it reminded him of his mother's sickness. Beneath the tattoos and the bad boy good looks, he was really a big softy, and so loveable.

"I'm not too sure. I gave her a ring but there was no answer so I'm on my way to see if she's home."

"Good, let me know how that goes. When you're done there you feel like swinging by to get me? We could pick up something for dinner and I can cook for you, for once."

"Mm, a man who cooks, now that's sexy." She chuckled. "What time you think you'll be done working?"

"Should be done with my last client by seven," he said.

"I'll see you then. Oh, and Mace…" She paused for a moment. "I'll bring the dessert. Whip cream, chocolate sauce, maybe some cherries you can eat off me. You have any preference?"

He cursed. "My favorite flavor is you, babe. Anything else is just icing on the cake."

"I'm missing you more and more as we speak." She teased. "See you as soon as I can okay?"

"Yeah, gotta go," he replied. "At work, stuck with a boner. Speaking to you isn't helping right now when all I can think about is getting you naked."

"Hmm, I'm so wet right now." She giggled when he growled. "Listen I just pulled into the driveway. Recite the alphabet backwards or think unsexy thoughts to help deflate your situation. I'll keep you posted on what's happening here."

"You do that, I lo…" Mace cleared his throat. "I'll see you soon."

"Definitely," she replied, "I love you too, Tattoos."

Becca had been sure he was about to say that to her, but he stopped himself for some reason and she just wanted to make sure that he knew she did too. Only she chickened out because she disconnected the call as soon as those meaningful words left her mouth. They'd talk about it when she saw him later. In the meantime, she had a sweet old lady to visit.

Becca sighed as she got out of her car and she touched her belly to calm her nerves. *Telling, Mace, you love him shouldn't be a big deal, right? Especially if he was about to say it first. But what if I was wrong? Rebecca Marie Everett, suck it up girl. Everything's bigger in Texas, from our hair to our pickup trucks. What's three little words?*

"The answer is—it's everything," she mumbled to herself as she climbed the steps to knock on the door. She took a deep breath and put all those thoughts to the back of her mind for now. As she stood in front of the door, she concentrated on the task at hand, which was to see how Mrs. Coulter was feeling. She'd be seeing her beloved boyfriend soon enough.

"Becca, what a pleasant surprise," Baxter answered her knock on the door and eagerly continued, "come in, come in." He swept his arm inside the house, motioning for her to enter so she did.

The Coulter place was much bigger than her own, and she couldn't help but be captivated by the beautiful structure. It was a large older Victorian style house with decorative banisters, high ceilings, and sleek woodwork throughout. "Thank you, Bax. You know I forgot how lovely this place is." She turned around and was startled by his proximity to her. He seemed to come out of his trance when she noticed he was in her space and he took a step back.

"Yes, well a house is a house."

She wasn't sure how to respond so she just went with the truth. "I stopped by to see how your Grams was doing. May I see her?" she asked.

"Of course," he said. "You wait right here, and I'll go see if she's up to it."

Becca watched Baxter's retreating form and appreciated her new-found personal space since he left to go upstairs. She still stood in the entryway and admired the family photos that adorned the walls. There were wedding photos, childhood ones, and self-portraits too. She particularly liked the one of the late Mr. Coulter in an army uniform smiling down at a younger version of the lady she was there to see. You could just feel the love they shared with that one photo alone. It was precious, and they were quite a handsome couple.

She was straightening the frame as Baxter rejoined her. "That picture was taken in 1958, right before they were married," he said, and she watched him as he twisted a white cloth between his fingers.

A handkerchief maybe?

"It's captivating," Becca replied. "They look so right for each other in it."

"Yes, my grandmother still talks about it like it was yesterday. I think she secretly wishes I'd find someone to settle down with." He went on.

"Well, maybe you should," Becca whispered. "Finding a good person to spend your time with is a gift. It's even better when you find love, but you won't achieve any of it if you don't put yourself out there. I would know. Until recently I was ready to give up on any romantic interests, but I've met someone and it's going great. You can have that too, Bax. I know you're taking care of your grandmother and busy with work, but you have to make time for you too."

"It's that guy with the tattoos, isn't it?" He snapped, "What's so great about him?"

She retreated as he advanced, and it brought her further into the house while he blocked the exit. She was uncomfortable now, if only she could make it to the back door to run away. "What? I-I came to visit with your Grams, not to upset you. I don't understand."

"I don't understand." He mocked. "There's only one interest I have, my sweet Becca, and if I can't have you, neither can he!" He lunged for her this time and it caught her off guard. She tried to twist around to escape him, but it backfired on her when he caught the move and tackled her to the ground. The table beside them wobbled and a few knickknacks on top smashed to the ground. Her struggles were futile as he put his full weight on top of her body, holding her in place on her stomach. She struggled with him some more as he was determined to hold the white cloth over her face. Becca tried bucking him off, and scratching at his arms but it was useless. Baxter was so much stronger and it only took but a few moments before everything went black and his plan was in motion.

***

Mace

"What time is Becca picking you up?" Sawyer asked.

"Any minute now." Mace looked at his watch as Sawyer flipped the sign on the door to closed. "Jagger coming to get you tonight?"

"Nah, he had a project to finish so I told him I'd just meet him at home." Jagger was Sawyers fiancé, and first love. After several misunderstandings and years apart, they had found each other again and had been together ever since. Mace was genuinely happy for his pseudo sister from another mister. Proud too, seeing as she'd come from hard times only to pull herself out of it and pursue her dream. Mad Ink was then created, and the tattoo parlor was a hit. Jagger on the other hand was a master welder. He built horse trailers mostly and decked them out with some pretty cool artwork as his signature touch. Each made was a one of a kind, which kept him busy. That's the current project he was working on as Sawyer had mentioned.

"Then do me a solid and wait until Becca gets here so I can walk you out and make sure you get to your car safely," he said. "I'll send Jag a text to let him know you may be a few minutes late."

"Whatever." Sawyer rolled her eyes. "You've been hogging Becca lately anyway, so it'll give me a chance to say hello."

"I have, haven't I?" he said and smiled. "Can't help myself."

"Aw, look at you." She laughed merrily. "I never thought I'd see the day. Brody Mace has met his match."

"She just told me she loved me," he confessed. "This afternoon on the phone, I was just about to say it and then chickened out. She must have figured it out because she just came out and said, 'I love you too, Tattoos.' And, then she hung up."

"I always liked that girl," Sawyer remarked. "So, do you?"

"Do I what?"

"Do you love her back?" she clarified.

"I'm pretty sure I do." He mumbled, "Think I'll tell her tonight."

"Oh yay!" Sawyer clapped and then gave him a huge hug. "I am so happy for you. You deserve greatness, Mace. After all you've been through, this is nice to see, and Becca's amazing. Beginning to think of her as a sister and now she will be thanks to you." She playfully punched him in the shoulder and smiled big.

"Thanks, squirt. It means a lot," he said, and looked at his watch again. "Hey, what time you got?"

Sawyer checked the time on her cell. "It's almost seven-thirty. Why?"

"That's what I thought," Mace replied. He stood up to look out the storefront window. "Becca was supposed to be here at seven. It's not like her to be late."

"So, give her a call," she suggested. "Maybe she got stuck in traffic."

"Doubtful, but anything's possible," he said, dialing her number. It rang several times before an automated operator came on to say she was unavailable now. Sawyer watched Mace pace in front of the window, and he got more anxious as the time approached eight o'clock. Becca was always on time, and very organized. This wasn't like her at all and something in his gut didn't feel right. He kept calling her and she wasn't answering.

"You think she went home? Maybe she thought she was supposed to meet you at your place?" Sawyer asked.

"Not sure, but I can't sit around here and twiddle my thumbs. I've gotta find her, Sawyer," he pleaded. "Think you can stick around and call Jag to pick you up? Becca drove me in, so I'll need to borrow your car."

"She's all yours." Sawyer dangled her keys for him to take them and sighed. "I know you're worried but try to think positive okay. The last thing anyone needs is for you to drive recklessly because you're worried and then you could hurt yourself or somebody else along the way. It's probably all a misunderstanding, so give Becca my love and tell her we need to make some plans to hang out soon, okay?"

"Okay," he said, and then he took a deep breath. "I'll call when I know something." Sawyer nodded and gave him a kiss on the cheek.

"If she shows here between now and the time Jagger gets here. I'll give you a call."

Mace was out the door and done with wasting any more time. It was time to find Becca, so he could tell her he loved her too.

He drove to her house, checked his place out, stopped by her office, and drove around the various spaces she owned and leased. He'd also knocked on the old lady's door, Becca's last known location with no luck. He then called Sawyer back to see if she'd heard anything. Hours had passed by with still no sign of her. His stomach sank with dread because there was no mistaking his initial gut instinct that something was very wrong here. His next stop was the police station, and afterwards he was going to round up everyone he knew to help him look, and he didn't plan on stopping until she was found safe and in his arms again.

"I love you, Becca, and I promise, baby, I will find you."

***

Becca

Her head ached, and her body felt heavy. Her cheek was pressed against a cold damp surface and she whimpered. *Where am I?* She went to put her hand to her forehead and met resistance. "What's happening to me?"

"It's nice to see you're finally awake," Baxter said, and the whole nightmare came crashing back. "But I had to tie you up to ensure you wouldn't try to leave me."

"Why?" she cried.

"Because you're mine." He growled. "I've been infatuated with you for years, but you never took notice. I even tried to enlist my grandmother to set us up knowing how much you respected her. But no, that didn't work so I bided my time. I then became interested in someone else. Oh, don't worry you still held my interest, but this new mysterious woman was every man's fantasy. A dream come true, so I was patient. You see, just like you, she was a hard-working woman who loved her family as she gave subtle but caring little hints about them in the stories she'd share. So, there was no doubt she was caring. But she was also a naughty girl, in the best way possible." He snickered. "What's that saying? A lady in the streets, but a whore between the sheets."

Baxter moaned when he said it and began to rub the front of his pants. There was no denying the outline of his hard cock there, and it made her cry harder not knowing what he was going to do next. Would he hurt her, rape her? She was at his mercy and scared shitless.

"Please, Bax. Don't do this," she begged. "Think of your Grams. She'd be so devastated to know you did this to me."

"I'm not finished!" he yelled. "So, listen up. You asked why, I'm telling you. Now, where was I? Oh, that's it, whore in the sheets. I fantasized as I read every word, stroked myself like this…" he said as he demonstrated for her, and she gagged in response. This man masturbating in front of her was a monster. She felt so violated already but he ignored her reaction and continued to explain as she now sat on the cold stone floor. "But it wasn't until I came across the Curious Minds post that I figured it out. You see, the woman I was fascinated with, who I fantasized about, was also the very same woman I was always infatuated with. She's you, my Becca, or should I call you Cowgirl Crazy's E?" He tapped his chin as if in thought. "Why is it you sign off with an 'E' every time? Is it for Everett? Your last name."

"No!" She shook her head in denial and she began to shake. This man was pure madness defined. She had to figure out a way to escape before anything worse happened to her. *Keep him talking, Becca. Bide your time. Mace must be looking for you. He knew where you were going.*

"Don't deny it." Baxter cackled. "I love it when they play hard to get."

She chose to ignore that. "Where am I? What did you give me?" Her lips were cracked, her throat was dry, and her head was pounding.

"We're in the basement." He sneered, "It was broad daylight and I didn't want to risk anyone seeing me lugging around an unconscious body. Thankfully this place is old and solid enough that it's soundproof from above. The best part, nobody will find you, there aren't many houses in Kerrville with a basement like mine."

"I bet they're looking. It's not too late to let me go. I could tell everyone it was all a misunderstanding. The last thing I want, or need, is to hurt your grandmother. Please, Bax, untie me."

"Shut up, just shut up!" he hollered and grabbed a chunk of her hair to yank her up from the ground. Her cuffs strained against her wrists and she hissed in pain when he yanked her forward. Spittle flew from his mouth and he got right into her face. "I told you you're mine. Mine to do whatever I please with, and you're going to stay here until I figure out our next move."

He cocked a fist and her head flew backward as he hit her in the face. Becca cried out and collapsed to the floor in a heap.

"You see what you did? Maybe next time you'll think twice about getting me angry. You'll learn to obey. Do what you're told. You wanted answers, I gave you some. Get used to this." His cell phone beeped, and he reached in his pocket to turn off the timer he'd set. "It's time for more of Gram's meds. I'll be back for you as soon as I can."

Baxter Bane Coulter left to go up the stairs to medicate his grandmother when she finally gained enough courage to answer him. She also wanted to test his theory of sound and whether anyone would be able to hear her. "I will never give in, Baxter. Mace is looking for me. He'll be coming, you hear me? You won't get away with this!" she screamed. "You won't!"

"Oh, but I already have." He stood by the only door and chuckled. "I'll be back to deal with you soon enough, and I'll show you what it's like to be with a real man." He grabbed at his junk lewdly and slammed the door behind him.

Becca shrank herself into a ball and sobbed. Her faith was dwindling. Baxter seemed confident, and all she could do was pray to God she'd be found before it was too late.

Chapter Seven

Mace

Sawyer was one step ahead of him, and he didn't know what he'd do without her. By the time he went to meet her at her place after going to the police station, she'd assembled the masses. It had only been a few hours since Becca went missing so there wasn't much the police could do but keep an eye out. If she wasn't back by morning then he planned to go back until something was done, but they had suggested he gather some people to help him look in the meantime if he was that worried.

Of course, he had been.

He knew Becca enough now to know she just wouldn't take off without a word. They'd made plans. She told him she loved him, for Christ's sake.

He believed her.

After thanking everyone for coming to his aid, Sawyer especially, he took a deep breath and gained control. Sawyer, Ava, and Lena were going to

Becca's house in case she showed up there until further notice. Jagger and Alex were going back to Mad Ink to search the perimeter, and Liam volunteered to accompany him back to the Coulter's.

"Thanks for helping out. I'd be a wreck without you guys," Mace admitted. "I know we're on the right track. I just feel like I'm missing something."

"We'll find her, man. Now buckle up." Liam had insisted on driving there, and he was too worked up to argue. He counted down the seconds until their arrival to pass the time. Within minutes they'd arrived, and there was still no sign of Becca or her car. His heart plummeted again, but he forged on.

"Looks like they might be sleeping." Liam observed. All the windows were dark, and it was quiet except for the crickets outside.

"I noticed," he replied. "We came all this way and still no sign of her. I say it's time for a wakeup call. She was on her way here last time I talked to her, said she was pulling in before she hung up. Somebody's gotta know something."

"You're right about that," Liam said as he jumped the stairs two at a time to the front porch. "We'll bang until somebody answers or calls the cops. Either way we'll be talkin' to somebody before the night is through. I got your back however this goes."

"We're going to find my girl," Mace declared, and he said it to motivate himself. *Here goes nothing.*"

The first time Liam knocked it was quiet. The second loud knock must have startled somebody inside because they heard something crash. It went quiet again and still nobody answered.

"You hear that?" Liam put his ear to the door.

"We've either scared them, or someone doesn't want our company so they're not answering."

"Does the old lady live alone? I'd bet scared is the reason if that's the case," Mace said, and he looked to his friend for an answer.

"Pretty sure the grandson moved in to help her out, so it could be the latter," he replied.

Shit!

Mace pounded on the door this time. "The hell you say? He came by Becca's couple of weeks ago, didn't get a good vibe. Guy has a thing for her, but she's not interested." He knocked more persistently. "I'm sick of waiting. I understand if you want to back off and leave me to it, but I'm kicking this door in and getting some answers. She has to be in there, and if not, I bet that fucker knows where she is."

He didn't wait for an answer and kept kicking until the door gave away. Liam was right behind him as he entered. "Said I'd help. I'm not leavin' you here to deal with this alone."

Mace nodded, as they looked around and noticed a few of the knickknacks overturned. Some of them had even shattered. "Looks like there was a struggle at some point." He tilted his head towards the mess. "You check down here and I'll investigate upstairs. Holler if you find anything."

Liam was already gone into another room by the time he made it to the stairs. His heart beat frantically and he began to sweat. Once he made it up, he tiptoed quietly to each room to look inside, his back to the wall. All was clear so far, he'd checked three rooms and one bathroom. There were only two left. He opened the next and found the old lady unconscious but breathing. He tried nudging her awake but there was no use. She wasn't responding. Just then the closet burst open and a man ran out down the hall. Mace was immediately in pursuit.

He was fast, but not fast enough. As they hit the stairs Mace took a giant leap and knocked the guy down. It was that fucker Baxter, the grandson.

"Where is she?" he demanded. The shithead just grinned at him.

"Who?" he replied, playing dumb.

"Becca was here. I was talking to her when she got here. Now she's missing. I repeat, where is she? You don't answer, and I'll have to beat some answers out of you," Mace growled, and shook him a little to rattle him.

Dude must have been off his rocker because he just laughed in his face and whispered, "I'll never tell."

"Liam?" Mace barked.

"Yeah, bro, I'm here." Baxter squirmed when Mace looked up to see his friend leaning against the wall across from him. "You seemed to have the situation under control, so I left you to it."

"Any luck?" he asked, sounding hopeful. He glanced at Baxter and scowled. "Fucker's not talking."

"Didn't have a chance to check everywhere before I heard the scuffle over here, came to check it out." Liam stood. "What do you want to do with him?"

Mace answered with a punch, and Baxter howled in pain.

Wait...

88

"Do you hear that? Hold him for me will ya?"

Liam complied. They could hear sirens in the background now getting closer, but Mace didn't care. The noise was faint, but he'd heard it. Right before he punched the guy in the face.

Baxter squirmed as if he was nervous. "You hear nothing but the police, you moron. You triggered the silent alarm when you broke in. I'm pressing charges and Becca will forget all about you once they throw your ass in jail."

"Shut up, man," Liam grumbled, putting him into a choke hold. "That should hold him."

He heard it again when Baxter finally quieted. It was coming from the wall, so he pressed his ear to it.

Help me, somebody please!

It was her. He was sure of it. "Where's the door?" he yelled, punching his way across the wall. Something clicked inside, and he found the camouflaged doorway leading down stairs.

"Becca!"

"Mace?" she cried, "Mace, I'm here. Please I'm over here." She sobbed while he ran down and it brought him to his knees.

He finally found her, thank God, but not unscathed. Her hands were bound to the wall, her wrists red and raw as if she was trying to escape unsuccessfully, her eyes were puffy from crying and one was almost swelled completely shut. "He hit you?"

Becca nodded. "He would've done much worse if you hadn't come. Please find the key to unlock me before he comes back."

"He won't be coming near you. Trust me?" he

asked, and she nodded through her tears.

"Yes, yes, I do." Her hands shook as she tried to reach out to him, and the chain rattled. He had just enough time to cup the sides of her face and press a gentle kiss to her head before the police came charging down to save the day.

Becca and Mrs. Coulter were both transported to the hospital, while Mace and Liam were held back to give statements. He couldn't wait to get out of there to be with her. He was able to call Sawyer to relay what happened and she headed straight there to be with Becca, so he was glad she wasn't alone. Mrs. Coulter was still out of it by the time EMT's arrived, she'd been drugged but would thankfully make a full recovery eventually. Becca was understandably shaken up but he admired her strength considering the circumstances. They were both safe now, that was all that mattered.

Baxter on the other hand was arrested, and with any luck they'd throw the book at him. It'd be a cold day in hell before he got out of jail and the bastard deserved every bad thing coming his way.

The hours felt like days before he was able to see her. They were keeping her for the day under observation. He walked in the door and Sawyer immediately got up to give him a hug. "She's sleeping," she whispered. "I'm heading out to get some sleep. Let me know if anything changes, will you?"

"Yeah," he agreed. He couldn't take his eyes off Becca's still form and he gulped down some of the emotion overwhelming him. He sat at her bedside and held her hand.

"Mace?" Somebody was shaking him, and he opened his eyes groggily.

"Huh?"

"They're discharging me soon, honey, wake up." Becca shook him again, and everything came rushing back. He jumped to his feet and gently gathered her inside his arms.

"Scared the shit outta me, Becca. I went crazy with worry." He whispered, "I never want to let you go."

"It scared the shit out of me too." She wiped a tear. "But you found me. I can never thank you enough for not giving up."

"I couldn't. I should have said so yesterday but I pussied out." He cupped her face again and looked her directly in the eye. "I love you, Becca, so fuckin' much baby. I need you to know it."

She began to cry harder at his admission and she inelegantly wiped her nose on her sleeve before she could reply. "I love you too, Mace."

Luckily, besides the trauma of the whole ordeal, Becca was finally able to leave the hospital with only a few bumps and bruises. Mace took it easy on her for a couple of weeks and doted on her hand and foot until Becca had enough.

***

Becca

"It's been three weeks, and four days since it happened, Mace. I'm okay now." She assured him. He still treated her as if she was fragile and although she loved him for it, enough was enough. Therapy was doing wonders for her, and she felt as if she was at a good place right now, at least for the day anyway. "Just love me."

"I do, sweetheart," Mace reassured her, pulling her closer to him.

She cuddled with him. "Show me." She turned around so that she was facing him and flicked his nipple. "I need you, big guy."

She didn't have to tell him twice. "Happy to be of service," he said, but she cut him off with a kiss. She could feel the solid form of his cock pressed against her and became desperate to have him. Becca climbed on top and ripped her tank off. Mace took the cue and helped her with her thong. Completely naked now, she ground against him without breaking the kiss. They were both breathless when she finally pulled back and yanked off his boxer briefs. Her breasts heaved as she admired what she had to work with. She loved his cock. She grabbed the base and placed him where she needed him. They moaned in unison when he entered her, and she cursed. It felt so good.

"Giddy up, babe." Mace smacked her on the ass and thrust up to go deeper.

"Oh, I'll ride you all right." She exclaimed, "Better than that damn bull."

"Hell, yeah, you will," he groaned, and she did as asked by riding him with all the energy she had. Their bodies were sweat slicked, and the only sounds in the room besides their moaning in pleasure were that of skin slapping skin before their orgasms erupted. Once Mace was close he played with her clit until she shouted from the roof tops. Her pussy quivered around him, the warm, silky vibrations causing him to explode inside of her.

It got better and better every single time.

She collapsed on top and he rubbed her back. He seemed content, so she just laid there listening to his heart beat for a few minutes to gather her thoughts. One thing she'd learned from this whole ordeal was that life was too short to go wasting time, and she knew what she wanted. He laid beneath her. "Tell Sawyer you appreciate her generosity, but you're giving her the house back."

"Say what?" Mace sounded shocked, so she repeated herself. This time she looked up and met his gaze.

"I love you, Mace. Tell Sawyer you're giving her the house back."

"That's what I thought you said," he replied. "And?"

"And, move in with me," she said, as she sat up. His flaccid dick started to inflate inside of her and she wiggled against him. "I know I want you, love you, and I miss when you're not around. Who cares what anyone thinks. Move in with me. Let's make this permanent."

Mace looked at her thoughtfully, and she bit her lip, suddenly nervous. "Well, don't leave me hanging."

"Hand me my phone," he said and held out his hand. Becca jumped off him and searched for his jeans. Once she located them, she searched his pockets until she found it. She silently handed it over and sat cross-legged beside him as he sat up in bed.

He dialed the phone and pressed it against his ear. "Hey, squirt, what you up to?"

He chuckled. "Yes, I know what time it is. Don't tell me you were sleeping."

"Uh huh."

"Ugh, TMI, brat."

"La, la, la…" he sang, and Becca giggled. Sawyer was awesome, and she loved watching Mace squirm sometimes.

"Okay, listen up. I'm giving the house back."

"Uh huh."

"I know, ya, ya, already. I promise to still help with fixing it up. It'll just be empty. I'm moving in with Becca."

"Of course, she's okay with this. It was her idea." He rolled his eyes. "Just a sec…"

"She wants to talk to you," Mace said and handed her the phone. He placed his hands behind his head and got comfortable.

"Hey, Sawyer,"

"He's moving in. I'm so happy for you!" Sawyer said it with such enthusiasm that Becca had to take the phone from her ear.

Mace chuckled and mouthed "I love you" to her silently.

Becca placed a hand to her heart and smiled. "I wanted something more permanent and he's giving it to me."

"I can't tell you how glad I am for you both." Sawyer continued. "Let me know when you want his stuff out of the house, and Jagger and I will help him move it into yours with the truck."

"Will do," Becca said.

"That's all she wrote. Gotta go, I've got a hot man waiting for my services. Later," Sawyer said and hung up as soon as Becca said, "Bye."

"She took it pretty well." Becca eyed the phone and handed it back to him.

"Knew she would." Mace grinned. "I'm moving in." He reached for her and pulled her on top of him again. He started kissing her and rolled them over so that he was on top now. He was hard as a rock and slid home to make love again. They took it slow this time, and Becca felt complete for the first time in a long time.

Epilogue

Mace

Sawyer and Jagger had just made it to the house. The three of them sat in the living room while Becca was still upstairs getting ready. They'd been living together officially for a couple of days and Sawyer wanted to go out and celebrate. Since they hadn't been out with the gang since the other couple's engagement party a few months back, Becca and Mace agreed.

They were meeting Liam and Ava at their bar shortly for drinks and dancing, but first they were waiting on Toby. They hadn't talked since Mace had first arrived in Kerrville, and he received a text last night to expect a call. Sawyer received the same.

Toby James was a famous tattooist, cousin to the rock prodigy Ash Harris who was lead singer of the band, Love the Sinner. Most importantly, he was like family to them as he was once engaged to Sawyer's sister and was there for Mace when he went through all that shit with taking care of and then losing his mom. Toby was also a survivor and Mace admired him for it even if the man himself didn't see himself that way. The phone rang, and he jumped to answer it. He put it on speaker and placed it on the coffee table.

"Toby, long time no speak," he greeted.

"Hey, man, Sawyer with you?" Toby asked.

"Sure am, big brother. How are you?" Sawyer replied.

"Hey, squirt, I'm hanging on. Jagger still treating you properly?"

"You can count on it." Jagger assured, and Sawyer smiled at him before she put her two cents in. "He's been great, Tob. We'll see you at the wedding, I hope."

"Wouldn't miss it." He said, "How about you, Mace? Meet any ladies who can stand your ugly mug yet?"

"Ha, ha," Mace mocked, "You know I've never had problems in that department, and I met the best one there is."

"It's true, Toby. You should see him. They're living together now, and he's all domesticated. It's a good look for him." Sawyer stuck out her tongue in Mace's direction and smiled. "Becca's a peach, you'll like her."

"Congrats." Toby chuckled over the receiver. "Never thought I'd see the day, but you deserve the happiness."

"Hey, thanks man," Mace replied, and he motioned Becca over as she descended the stairs.

"Hi, Toby, I'm Becca, Mace's girlfriend. I've

heard so much about you, all good things of course."

"I'm sure you did," Toby said, and you could hear the smile in his voice. "Nice to meet you, Becca."

"Likewise, Toby."

"How are things with the shop? And, your love life? You deserve just as much happiness as the rest of us. Carley would have wanted it that way," Sawyer whispered the last part and swallowed.

"Shop's you know, same old, same old. Hired a new guy named Rebel, he's good too and we're as busy as ever. As for the other stuff, met someone, scared the shit outta me and I fucked it up. Trying to make it right though, so wish me luck. Have a feeling I'll need it." Toby sighed. "The gang gives you their love."

"Well, then give them ours back," Sawyer said, and she leaned closer to the upturned cell phone on the table. "Good luck, Toby, it'll work out. What's her name?"

"Harlow," he said, then sighed. "You really think Carley would be okay with this?" Sawyer's sister had died in a fire and Toby had dealt with survivor's guilt because he survived, and she didn't. She never questioned how much he loved her though, and she knew in her heart her sister loved him enough that she'd want him to move on and be happy with his life.

"I know it, Toby. Harlow must be something special to bring all this up, so do what you have to do to fix whatever you did and make it right. It's an order."

"We'll see." He sighed again. "I'll keep you posted."

"You do that, man," Mace said, "and, next time don't wait so long to call."

"I'll call you next week," Sawyer blurted. "We love you, bro."

"Yeah, love you too, baby girl. Listen I gotta go. Clients coming in and then I have to figure out a way to get Harlow to talk to me. Maybe Mel will help me out," he muttered. "They're friends."

"Good luck, Tob," Mace said.

"Bye, man," Jagger said after him, Becca stayed quiet, and then Sawyer spoke her peace.

"We'll talk soon, and you know how to reach me if you need anything. We're out."

***

Becca

"Well that was interesting." Becca observed. "Sounds to me like he may finally be healing."

"Yeah," Sawyer agreed. "It'll be interesting to see how it goes with this Harlow woman. She must be something special to have Toby tied in knots like this. Good for him." She stood and clapped her hands. "Yet another thing to celebrate tonight. Let's go get our drink on."

And so, they did.

They drank, they danced, toasted their happiness, and celebrated new found love with great friends at Tipsy's.

They were sitting at the table again when Mace pulled Becca's chair closer to his and he held on to her belt loop. He leaned in close and whispered in her ear while everyone else talked around them, "Whatch'ya thinking about?"

Becca shivered with goose bumps as his breath caressed over her ear when he spoke. "I'm eyeing that mechanical bull over there. Care to make a new wager?"

"Hell yeah!" Mace exclaimed, and he perked right up, gaining the attention of everyone at the table. "What do you have in mind?"

"Same terms as last time, we both ride and whomever lasts the longest wins. Jagger's our time keeper. You win, and I'll let you have your pick of the toy box."

"You win, and I'll wash the dishes for a week," he interrupted.

"Dishes for a week, and I get to have my way with you. I'm talking about being in charge in the bedroom. You do as I say, and I promise to make it worth your while," she whispered back.

Mace smiled. "Either way, and I'm a winner in my book."

"I feel the same way." She chuckled, and then stood. "The bet's on again, ladies, and I'm riding first."

As everyone followed them to the bull, she watched Mace's tight ass in front of her while he led the way, and she knew without a doubt all was right in her world.

The End

If you enjoyed reading *Chasing Butterflies*, and *Cowgirl Crazy,* stay tuned for the *Misfit Tattoo* series in the near future. Toby James's story, *Forever With You*, is coming soon…

***

Also, don't forget to consider leaving a review. It's greatly appreciated.

Thank you!

About the Author

Jennifer Labelle resides in Canada with her husband and three beautiful children. After her third child she became a stay at home mom. In her busy household Jennifer likes to spend her down time engrossed in the stories that she creates. She is an active reader of romance, mystery and anything paranormal. With an education in Addictions work she's decided to take a less stressful approach in life and hopes that you enjoy, as she shares some of her imagination and artistic inspiration with all of you.

Facebook:
https://www.facebook.com/pages/Author-Jennifer-Labelle/168414043184292

Twitter:
https://twitter.com/1JenniferLabell

Goodreads:
https://www.goodreads.com/author/show/4649930.Jennifer_Labelle

Website:
http://www.jenniferlabelle.com/

Google Plus:
https://plus.google.com/u/0/110192794885898998367/posts

BookBub:
https://www.bookbub.com/profile/jennifer-labelle

Join our Reader Group on Facebook and don't miss out on meeting our authors and entering epic giveaways!

Limitless Reading

Where reading a book
is your first step to becoming
limitless...

LIMITLESS PUBLISHING *Reader Group*

Join today! *"Where reading a book is your first step to becoming limitless..."*

https://www.facebook.com/groups/Limitless Reading/